A GHOSTLY ALMANAC OF DEVON & CORNWALL

A GHOSTLY ALMANAC OF
OF
DEVON &
CORNWALL

NICOLA SLY

The
History
Press

First published 2009

The History Press
The Mill, Brimscombe Port
Stroud, Gloucestershire, GL5 2QG
www.thehistorypress.co.uk

British Library Cataloguing in Publication Data.
A catalogue record for this book is available from the British Library.

ISBN 978 0 7524 5268 5

Typesetting and origination by The History Press
Printed in Great Britain

CONTENTS

ACKNOWLEDGEMENTS

As always, there are numerous people to be thanked for their assistance, especially those people who were prepared to share their stories and who gave their permission for me to include them in this book. Many of them asked to remain anonymous and, throughout the book, these people have been allocated pseudonyms. Readers are respectfully reminded that many of the places described in the book are private residences and are asked to observe the privacy of the owners and current occupiers.

I must thank Melanie Crawford, whose skilful drawings brought some of the featured ghosts to life, and Kim Van der Kiste for supplying the photograph of Bodmin Gaol. I must also thank Matilda Richards, my editor at The History Press, not least for the many sleepless nights that I have spent in the company of the ghosts of Cornwall and Devon while compiling this book. My husband, Richard, was, as always, a great help in proof reading each chapter. A confirmed sceptic on all things paranormal, even he struggled to find a rational explanation for some of the phenomena detailed within the following pages.

ALSO BY THE AUTHOR

Bristol Murders
Cornish Murders (with John Van der Kiste)
Dorset Murders
Hampshire Murders
Murder by Poison
Shropshire Murders
Somerset Murders (with John Van der Kiste)
West Country Murders (with John Van der Kiste)
Wiltshire Murders
Worcestershire Murders

INTRODUCTION

In the past, I have written several factual books on historical murders and it was at a meeting with my editor about one such book that the conversation turned to the subject of ghosts. Given that I spend so much of my time researching and writing about sudden, violent deaths, I was asked whether or not I believed in the existence of ghosts and my reply was that I had a completely open mind on the subject – I neither believed nor disbelieved, even though I once lived in a house said to be haunted and had seen and heard several things that seemed to defy rational explanation. Then, while researching for another book, I came across an intriguing photograph. In August 1908, Mrs Luard was brutally murdered on the veranda of her summerhouse in Sevenoaks, Kent. Although her husband was a strong suspect, he later committed suicide and the murder remains unsolved to this day. Look at the photograph of the scene of the murder – is the ghostly figure on the centre of the balcony simply a trick of the light or a manifestation of the victim from beyond the grave?

The scene of the Luard murder, Sevenoaks, 1908. (Author's collection)

It was agreed that I would look objectively at some of the reputedly haunted sites of Devon and Cornwall with the purpose of trying to substantiate some of the accounts and compiling a collection of 'true' ghost stories from the region.

In the course of my research for this book, I have found many reports that can immediately be discounted as either false or grossly exaggerated. For example, I found a public building in Devon that was supposedly haunted by the ghost of a little girl who had died there many years earlier as a result of a tragic fire. By looking back to the contemporary newspaper reports of the incident, I discovered that the only victims had been three chickens. Conversely, a fire at a theatre in Exeter in 1887, in which more than 100 people tragically lost their lives, seems to have produced no verifiable cases of ghosts or haunting.

Numerous pubs and hotels throughout the region claim to be haunted, usually by the ghost of a historical murder victim. However compelling these accounts seem to be at first glance, I did not include them unless I could verify that a murder had actually taken place. The one exception to this rule was the notorious Jamaica Inn on Bodmin Moor, where the reports of ghosts are so consistent and well documented over the years that I felt that it merited inclusion.

However sceptical I might have been when I began writing this book, many of the reported sightings of ghosts in Devon and Cornwall seemed to be supported by the examination of historical records, including contemporary newspapers and censuses. I can also say with absolute honesty that every single person who was prepared to allow me to recount their personal experiences was unshakeable in his or her belief that they had witnessed at first-hand some form of paranormal activity.

I made a deliberate point of avoiding reading any books on the subject of ghosts before I had completed my research, which was thus mainly drawn from historical newspaper accounts. These are listed in more detail in the bibliography at the end of the book.

Now, more than a year after the subject of ghosts was initially raised in casual conversation, having spoken to many people about their experiences, my own attitude to ghosts has changed somewhat and I find myself more convinced about the existence of a 'life' beyond the grave. I will leave you to draw your own conclusions . . .

Nicola Sly, 2009

JANUARY

North Devon District Hospital, Barnstaple, Devon

Given that many people will have died in hospitals over the years, the odd tale of ghostly activities in these institutions is perhaps not altogether surprising.

Jackie was admitted to the North Devon District Hospital early in 1996 with a very high temperature. She was immediately placed in isolation in a private room. Jackie freely admits to being delirious and to having hallucinations at the height of her fever, the most vivid of which being that there was a young boy standing pressed against the wall in the corner of the room. Even years later, she vividly remembers him as being about five or six years old, with a sad, flushed face and dark, wavy hair. He was wearing striped pyjamas and looked absolutely terrified at the activity that was taking place around Jackie's bed, as the nurses battled to bring down her temperature. Ill though she was, Jackie recalls feeling that it was most important to reassure the frightened little boy and remembers trying to persuade the nurses looking after her to comfort him.

It would be all too easy to dismiss Jackie's experiences as the product of her illness – except for two strange occurrences.

When Jackie's fever had dropped, the nurses caring for her asked if she could remember her 'hallucination', which she still found upsetting several days later. Having described the little boy she had seen in the room, she was shocked when one of the nurses told her that a child exactly matching her description of the little boy had died there just a few weeks earlier.

Then, some years later, Jackie was at a dinner party in her home village in North Devon when the conversation turned to ghosts. To Jackie's surprise, one of the guests began to relate a story of being in a private room at the North Devon District Hospital and of waking from a nap to find a small boy, dressed in striped pyjamas, standing in her room 'looking lost'. When she spoke to him, the little boy immediately faded away and she had assumed that she had simply dreamed the encounter.

Jackie and her fellow dinner guest were quickly able to establish that both of them had been in the same private room at the hospital within three weeks of each other during January 1996 and that both had apparently seen the same little boy in exactly the same place.

Braddon Down, Near Lostwithiel, Cornwall

On 19 January 1643, Braddon Down near Lostwithiel was the site of a battle in the English Civil War. Royalist forces, commanded by Sir Ralph Horton, had spent the previous night camped at Boconnoc. As they were decamping, they discovered a contingent of Parliamentarian cavaliers preparing to challenge them.

In a battle that lasted for approximately two hours, the Royalists managed to defeat the Parliamentarian contingent without too much difficulty, effectively placing the county of Cornwall back under Royalist control.

The anniversary of the battle is said to be marked each year by the thunder of phantom hoof beats.

Brixham, Devon

On 9 January 1975, actor John Slater died in the National Heart Hospital after a long illness.

Although he appeared in many films, television programmes and stage plays throughout his career, Slater was perhaps best remembered for his role in the long-running television programme *Z Cars*, in which he played the character Detective Sergeant Stone. John and his wife, Betty, had a home in Brixham for many years and, while living in the town, they took an active interest in the theatre there. Slater was even credited with personally saving the theatre when it was threatened with closure by taking out a lease on the building.

Slater is reputed to haunt both the theatre and also the rehearsal rooms of the Brixham Operatic and Dramatic Society at Cavern Hill. Since his death, there have been numerous sightings of Slater in costume at the theatre, along with reports of unexplained malfunctions of equipment, including the stage curtains. On occasions, a performance has been cancelled because the curtains refused to open, only for them to inexplicably be in perfect working order again as soon as the cancellation was announced.

Royal Devon and Exeter Hospital, Exeter, Devon

In 1741, Dr Alured Clarke was appointed Dean of Exeter and immediately set about providing the city with a new, modern hospital. He approached local landowner John Tuckfield and managed to secure the donation of a large piece of land in Southernhay, which had previously been used for holding fairs and horse shows. Once he had the site for his new hospital, Dean Clarke commissioned architect John Richards to design the building.

On 1 January 1743, Mary Coote and John Elliot became the first outpatients to be treated at the new hospital, with the first in-patients being admitted just days later. The hospital was awarded royal status after a visit from the Duke and Duchess of York in 1899.

Above: *Brixham. (Author's collection)*

Left: *John Slater, 1970s. (Author's collection)*

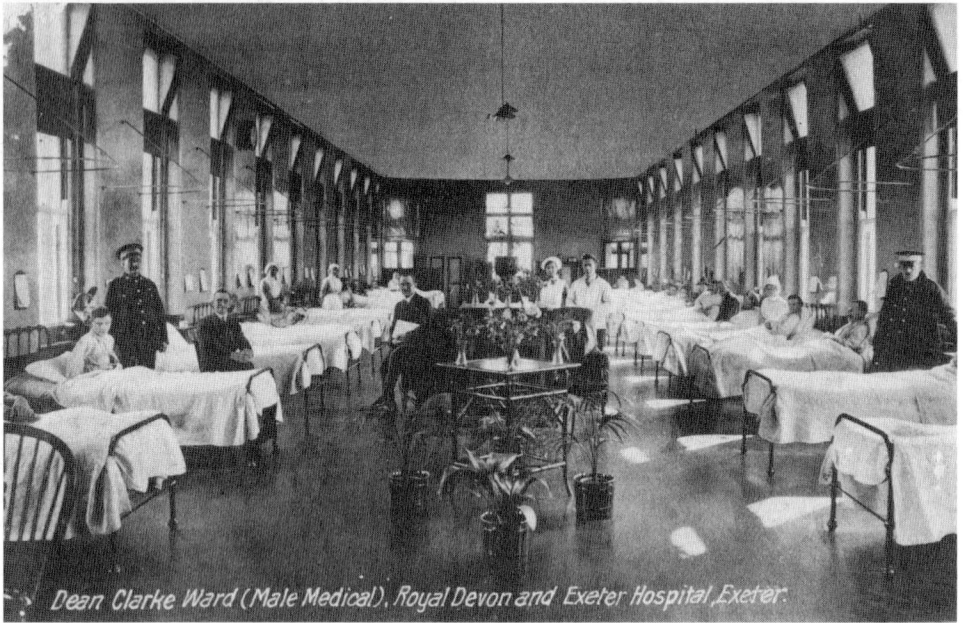

Dean Clarke Ward (Male Medical), Royal Devon and Exeter Hospital, Exeter.

Main Entrance, Royal Devon and Exeter Hospital, Exeter.

Top: *A ward at the Royal Devon and Exeter Hospital, 1950s. (Author's collection)*

Above: *The Royal Devon and Exeter Hospital, c. 1910. (Author's collection)*

Opposite: *An Exeter nurse. (Author's collection)*

However, by 1974, the old building had become woefully inadequate for supplying the medical needs of a large city and its surrounding areas and a new hospital was built in nearby Wonford. When the doctors and nurses finally moved out of the old hospital, they left behind the 'Grey Lady'.

So named because of her grey nurse's uniform, thought to date back to the eighteenth century, the Grey Lady frequently appeared on a corridor where the matron's sleeping quarters were located. She was usually seen running along the corridor, often inexplicably vanishing into thin air.

In researching this book, I spoke to a former patient at the hospital who, in the 1960s, was recovering from an operation and had unexpectedly developed a high temperature. She vividly recalls an 'old-fashioned' nurse, dressed in a grey uniform, leaning over her bed one night and placing a welcoming cool hand on her forehead.

At the time, her experience was dismissed as delirium due to her raised temperature. Yet, to the patient, the experience was very real indeed and her description of the nurse clearly describes a woman in eighteenth-century uniform – did she meet the famous Grey Lady?

Penzance, Cornwall

On 8 February 2001, the *Western Morning News* included a letter from a gentleman named Paul from Redruth.

Paul related his experiences during a late-night visit made to the cemetery in Penzance, which he made with a friend in January 2001. Although their visit to the cemetery 'started as a joke', what Paul and his friend both saw left them petrified.

Both men saw a strange white shape, like a person, floating over the ground in the cemetery. The apparition stayed in view for about a minute then disappeared as suddenly as it had appeared.

In his letter to the newspaper, Paul says that he and his friend were completely sober at the time and that neither of them believed in ghosts. Describing his sighting as 'quite unbelievable' he writes that he is aware of reports of other local people having seen 'something' at the cemetery.

Indeed, Paul's experience seems to be the latest in a long line of sightings of the apparition at the cemetery, which lies in an area dubbed 'The Penzance Triangle'. According to the results of a survey published in 2005, conducted by ghost researcher Lionel Fanthorpe, the 226-square-mile area of Cornwall between Land's End, St Ives and the Helford Estuary is among the most paranormally active areas of Britain.

Warleggan, Cornwall

The rectory adjacent to the church at Warleggan was a large, sprawling house set in about three-and-a-half acres of grounds, which were filled with beech trees and mature rhododendron bushes. In 1931 it was occupied by the Revd Frederick W. Densham, the new vicar.

Densham was not a local man and from the moment he took up his position in the parish, he and the villagers did not get on. One of his first acts was to purchase a litter of puppies, the largest of which he named Gandhi. As the puppies grew into dogs, they were allowed to roam free and took to hunting the surrounding moors in a pack. Several sheep were maimed and killed by Densham's dogs and, as a result, many of the local farmers stopped attending the church, while others demanded that the dogs should be destroyed. Eventually a compromise was reached and it was agreed that the rectory should be securely fenced to keep the animals confined. It was a mammoth project, but within a few months the rectory was sheltered behind an 8ft tall barbed-wire fence.

Densham's alienation of his congregation continued. At meetings of the Parochial Church Council he proposed several radical ideas, which were invariably greeted with stunned silence and suspicion by the villagers. His authoritarian insistence that his motions for improvement were carried caused further ill feeling amongst his parishioners.

Gradually the congregation in the tiny church dwindled to only a very few stalwarts, at which time Densham decided to paint the interior of the church in bold reds, yellows and blues. He did not consult his parishioners first; no doubt wanting to give them what he imagined would be a lovely surprise. The horror of the villagers when they saw their beautiful church so desecrated probably came as a surprise to Densham – but not a pleasant one. The remnants of the congregation voted on his interior design ideas with their feet and Densham found himself left with an empty church, week after week.

Matters came to a head in 1933, when the villagers complained to Dr Walter Frere, the Bishop of Truro, begging him to remove Densham from the parish. Frere suggested a meeting between the parishioners and Densham and, for once, Densham stood before a full church.

The villagers had five main complaints about their vicar to put to the bishop: he had stopped holding Sunday school, he refused to hold services at convenient times, he had threatened to sell the church organ, had converted church property for his own personal use, and had erected a barbed-wire fence around the rectory. The church secretary had another more personal grievance – he told the bishop that Densham had written to him threatening to kill him, after he had tried to prevent the priest tearing up the church.

The bishop assured the villagers that Densham had fulfilled his duties of office and therefore could not legitimately be removed from the parish. He urged them to show a Christian spirit and to make a fresh start. Yet there was no forgiveness to be found in the hearts of the villagers and, as one, they deserted the church.

Densham became somewhat of a recluse. Barricaded in the rectory behind his barbed-wire fence, he emerged only to attend church. Having no congregation, it was said that he filled the pews with cardboard cut outs of past rectors of the church

Warleggan Church. (© N. Sly)

to represent his missing flock. Then, having preached his sermons to an empty church each week, he would frequently visit the Methodist chapel where he would urge the congregation there to stay away from such activities as visiting the cinema, reading novels or playing whist. He had a particular dislike of smoking and would often admonish people for indulging in what he believed was a disgusting habit.

At the onset of the Second World War, Densham became even more isolated. He had raised the fence at the entrance of the rectory to a height of 12ft so that any callers had to announce their arrival by banging on the empty petrol drum that he kept at the gates. He received very few callers, with the exception of a grocer from Bodmin who made a fortnightly delivery of oats, cheese, butter and margarine, which were left just inside the rectory gates. Densham did not shun visitors through choice and made several attempts to let rooms to lodgers. However, when they saw the state of the rectory, which had no electricity or running water and was gradually falling into a state of disrepair, any potential applicants left without taking up the offer of a room.

One man did at least stay overnight. Densham wrote to a choir school in the Midlands, stating that he had a vacancy for an organist. Yet when the man arrived and saw the state of his accommodation and realised that there would be no church choir to work with and no congregation to listen to his music, he hurriedly left the next morning.

Densham had been advised by the bishop to focus on the young people of the area in an attempt to win the approval of their parents and, throughout his incumbency, he never ceased trying to gain the support of the village children. He habitually carried sweets in his pocket, which he would offer to them but, not surprisingly, the children's parents had warned them about taking anything from him. Now he converted part of the rectory grounds into a playground with a swing, roundabout, sandpit and a cemented boating pool. His efforts were shunned by the local children, as was a series of magic lantern slide shows that he planned for them.

Thinking that he might accept wartime evacuees into the rectory, Densham went to considerable effort to refurbish the rooms with bunkbeds and built-in cupboards and shelves. In anticipation of the children's arrival, he also purchased a chip fryer and a large quantity of potatoes. His work was inspected by the authorities who later wrote to him stating that, since there was no woman available to look after the children, they could not consider the rectory as a suitable billet for evacuees.

Now completely ostracised by all but a very few of the locals Densham set about transforming the rectory into a representation of the Bible lands, each room decorated to represent a particular area. Although he continued to preach at the church, his entries in the Church Register invariably documented 'No congregation attended.'

This was the case at Christmas in 1952, when his sermon 'God is Love' was, as usual, delivered to an empty church. However, in the new year, he unexpectedly found himself with an audience for his sermon on 'Level-headedness'. The strangeness of his situation in the small community of Warleggan had finally attracted the attention of the outside world and two journalists attended his church service with a view to writing articles about him. One came from the local paper, the *Western Morning News*, while the other came from further afield, representing the American magazine *Life*. Two days later, Densham died.

Shortly after the visit from the two journalists, villagers realised that they could no longer see smoke issuing from the rectory chimneys. Their banging on the petrol drum at the rectory gates elicited no response from within, so the police were called. When officers broke into the rectory, they found eighty-three-year-old Frederick Densham lying dead on the landing. He had obviously realised that death was fast approaching and had tried to get to his bedroom to die in bed but had not made it. His last act before death had been to pile apples on a table with labels indicating that they should be distributed among those villagers who were ill.

Just one solitary mourner attended Densham's funeral – his solicitor. The reverend's request to be cremated and have his ashes scattered in the rectory garden was ignored and instead they were scattered in the official Garden of Remembrance in Plymouth. In accordance with Densham's wishes, no memorial marked his last resting place.

The church at Warleggan was whitewashed and the rectory sold. However, the ghost of Frederick Densham is still said to walk the path between the former rectory and the church and there are reports of ghostly activities in the former rectory, which is now divided into flats. Undoubtedly a well-meaning man, he appears in death to continue to seek the approval of a community that had shunned him in life for his unapproachable and unbending ways.

FEBRUARY

Rosevear, Scilly Isles

On 24 February 1784, the East India Co. packet ship *Nancy*, bound from Bombay to London, sank in a raging storm off the Isles of Scilly with the resultant loss of the lives of her entire crew and thirteen passengers.

Among these was Ann Cargill, the most successful actress of her day who, up until the day of her death, had led such a scandalous life that her outrageous behaviour had prompted questions in Parliament. Indeed, having been a great success in India, she was only leaving that country because the then Prime Minister, William Pitt the Younger, had demanded that she should be deported on the grounds that 'an actress should not be defiling the pure shores of India.'

Cargill was born plain Ann Brown, the daughter of a coal merchant from London and made her stage debut at Covent Garden in 1771, at the age of eleven. She soon became a star, taking the lead part in numerous operas and musicals until she met and ran away with a celebrated playwright and gunpowder manufacturer, Miles Peter Andrews.

As she was still very young, her father sought to make her a ward of court, but she defied him and ran off again, returning to her meteoric career as a singer. Once, when her father tried to seize her outside a theatre, her fans thwarted his attempts.

In 1779, Ann eloped to Edinburgh with a Mr Cargill, returning to the stage as a married woman and becoming the highest paid actress in the world, receiving the then almost unheard of sum of £10 a week for her performances. At the height of her fame, she found another lover and eventually fled to India to join him. However, it was rumoured at the time that she was also enjoying a romance with ship's captain John Haldane, who also captained the *Nancy* on her tragic last voyage.

The storm of 1784 raged for a whole week, making any rescue attempt in the wake of the wreck impossible. When a boat was finally put out to check for survivors, all that was found were the battered and much mutilated bodies of the crew who had been dashed against rocks by heavy seas for several days. However, two bodies were surprisingly found virtually unscathed – those of a young woman and the baby clutched tightly in her arms.

The remains of all of the recovered bodies were hastily buried in makeshift graves on the uninhabited island of Rosevear. However, when paperwork from the wreck washed up onto the beaches was retrieved and sent to London, it was established that the young woman had been none other than the nation's favourite actress, Ann Cargill. Her body was immediately exhumed and buried in St Mary's.

Yet her spirit seems to have remained on Rosevear. Workmen who lived on the island while constructing the Bishops Rock Lighthouse in the 1850s reported a number of ghostly happenings and there have also been reports of the sound of a baby crying and of a woman's voice sweetly singing a lullaby.

South Devon

During the night of 7 February 1855, a heavy snowfall blanketed the whole of South Devon. Villagers throughout the area awoke to a world that had turned completely white overnight – and they also woke to something even stranger, the cause of which continues to remain a mystery to this day.

Something, or someone, had left a trail of footprints in the snow that stretched for more than 100 miles from Topsham through to Totnes. The prints were shaped like long, narrow hoof prints and appeared to have been made by a two-legged, rather than a four-legged creature.

The prints zigzagged across the county in a series of straight lines and, at one place, had even spanned the River Exe, stopping at one bank and then continuing on the opposite bank, as if whoever or whatever had made them had forded the river.

The prints went over roofs, through narrow drainpipes and even seemed to have passed through solid walls, stopping at one side and continuing on the other, leaving the snow on top of the walls undisturbed. Occasionally, the trail of prints stopped dead, continuing after a short break. Each footprint was uniformly sized, being about 4in long and 2½in wide, the distance between them a more or less constant 8½in. The occasional one looked to have been made by a cloven hoof. Several times the tracks went right up to the doorways of houses before turning away again.

Dr Benson of Mamhead followed one particular set of tracks across fields to a haystack, which was around 20ft high. The tracks stopped abruptly at the base but, when Benson went round to the other side, the footprints continued on across the fields as though whatever had made them had climbed, jumped over or walked straight through the haystack.

The local clergymen were quick to explain the phenomena as the Devil walking the countryside in search of sinners. Some believed that the prints were indisputable evidence of the existence of ghosts. Others sought more worldly explanations.

A kangaroo that had recently escaped from a private zoo in Sidmouth was initially believed to be the most likely culprit – until it was pointed out that the prints bore absolutely no resemblance to a kangaroo's tracks. It was then suggested that the footprints had been those of hungry badgers, forced by the snow to range across the county in search of food. Swans, rats, raccoons and otters were also suggested as the culprits, but none of the explanations that centred on wildlife could account for the fact that the tracks had been observed over such a great distance. A hot air balloon with a trailing rope was suggested, but how a rope could have trailed up to a wall and then continued on the other side without somehow disturbing the snow on the top of the wall was never satisfactorily explained.

The 'Devon Affair' was reported in *The Times* on 16 February 1855. The article stated that a group of armed men had set out from Dawlish to track down the maker of the peculiar prints but, as the newspaper commented wryly, 'As might be expected, the party returned as they went.' However, the newspaper coverage did bring forth accounts of similar events, both in Britain and in other countries, including one on 19 July 1205, when similar hoof prints in soft earth were reported following a fierce electrical storm.

It was eventually deemed to be a mystery that was unlikely ever to be solved unless it occurred again. However, on 16 January 1968, *The Times* revisited the story, discussing an explanation forwarded by Mr Alfred Leutscher of Essex.

Naturalist Leutscher was an expert on animal footprints and his theory was that mice had made the trail of prints. He explained his reasoning by demonstrating that when animals jump, they land on all 4 feet and, in soft, melting snow, the impression of their bodies would form a U-shape – a 'devil's footprint'. The only wild animal in this country small enough to make such a track would be the wood mouse, which are abundant in the countryside and Leutscher insisted that he had seen wood mouse prints in Epping Forest that corresponded exactly to the ones seen in Devon in 1855.

Leuthscher's explanation was accepted as a likely one by scientists and zoologists, although critics pointed out that the tracks covered more than 100 miles, an impossible distance for so small an animal to cover. Fairly obviously, more than one animal was involved and, since a wood mouse can climb and leap, it seemed a probable solution to the mystery. Yet why would a wood mouse climb over house roofs? Could it ford a river, or was the alleged river crossing performed like a relay race, with one mouse setting off cross-country as another reached the opposite bank?

The year 2009 saw the heaviest snow fall in Devon and Cornwall for many years and, on 12 March, *The Western Morning News* reported an incidence of similar footprints in Woolsery, North Devon. Reporter Louise Vennells related the appearance of a mysterious trail of single-track prints, which approached a house door and then crossed the garden, before vanishing into an area of relatively sparse snow coverage.

The homeowner called in a representative of the Centre for Fortean Zoology, who theorised that the hoof-shaped prints may have been made by either rabbits or hares, hopping on their hind legs. However, several readers subsequently contacted the newspaper with the suggestion that the prints were made by a fox.

Whereas these explanations seem perfectly reasonable today, they fail to explain the observations of 1855, at which time the prints appeared to climb over roofs and pass through narrow drainpipes and solid objects such as walls and haystacks, with no disturbance to the snow on the top of the obstacles. So many years after the 'Devon Affair', it is now unlikely that a satisfactory explanation will ever be found – unless, of course, there is a recurrence of the phenomena . . .

Tonacombe Manor, Cornwall

Tonacombe Manor near Morwenstow is a fifteenth-century house, formerly the estate of the Kempthorne family, and for many years sightings of several different ghosts have been reported, both in the house itself and in its surrounding fields.

One of these is believed to be the ghost of Katherine Kempthorne, who died at the manor on 12 February 1613, which is thought to appear annually on the anniversary of her death. Several residents have reported strange knocking noises, like the sound of a person knocking on the door. Others have awoken in the middle of the night to see strange misty figures standing at the end of their beds apparently watching them.

A former owner of the property described one such apparition as that of an elderly lady dressed in Tudor costume, whose lips were moving as if she were talking, although she made no sounds.

Others describe another ghostly presence; that of a small, balding man, dressed in a black coat, waistcoat and breeches that buttoned to the knee. In addition, a woman, presumed to be a housekeeper, has been seen standing by a fireplace with a large bunch of keys.

Dogs and cats have also been said to behave strangely in the area, often staring fixedly at something unseen by human eyes.

When it became known that I was researching this book, a farmer who farms close to the manor told me that on two separate occasions he had seen a man leaning on a field gate watching his tractor in apparent amazement. He described him as looking like a farm labourer, wearing a long, oversized brown smock and boots with gaiters. The same farmer has also heard the unmistakeable sound of horse's hooves galloping in the surrounding fields, when there were no horses in the area.

Week St Mary, Cornwall

Eighty-five-year-old Arthur related his experiences of owning a haunted holiday home in the village of Week St Mary during the 1970s and '80s. His daughter, now in her fifties, was with us while he recounted his story and confirmed his accurate recall of the salient details:

> Although we lived in the Midlands, we loved Cornwall and, from 1966 onwards, I took at least two, often more, holidays here each year with my wife and daughter. A small legacy that we received in the 1970s enabled us to realise our dream of buying a holiday home in the area.
>
> I eventually bought a property without my wife having seen it. On a visit to Cornwall with my elderly father, I fell in love with a cottage in Week St Mary and put in an offer with the estate agent. The offer was accepted and thus the first time that my wife saw the house was on the day we completed the purchase.

The cottage had been unoccupied for some time and, although it was structurally sound, it was badly in need of redecoration. As I had hoped, my wife also fell in love with the property and was soon brimming over with ideas about colour schemes, carpets, curtains and furniture.

We first visited the cottage together in February, intending to stay in a hotel for a couple of days, look around the cottage at our leisure and make some concrete plans for the renovations. However, we were thwarted by the weather. While we were in Cornwall, heavy snowfalls in the Midlands made the roads almost impassable for several days and, rather than risk driving home in such poor conditions, we elected to extend our stay and 'rough it' for a few nights at our new home.

On our first night there, my wife got up in the early hours to use the toilet. As she walked into the large bathroom, which had once been a bedroom, she was startled to see an old woman sitting there, in front of the window. My wife let out a huge shriek and rushed back to wake me up. By the time I went into the bathroom, it was empty and I managed, with some difficulty, to convince my wife that she had simply had a bad dream.

This was all very well, except that the old lady took to appearing in the bathroom at all hours of the day and night. Although there was no actual chair in the room, her faint form was always in a sitting position before the window. My wife and I both saw her on several occasions and were able to describe her as being very elderly with thinning grey hair gathered into a bun at the nape of her neck. She wore a high-necked, grey dress with buttons all the way down the front.

The snow in the Midlands finally cleared sufficiently for us to risk the journey home and, as we drove, my wife and I agreed on one thing – we would not mention the old lady to our daughter, who was then about twelve years old. She was a child with a very vivid imagination and we didn't want to frighten her. What we hadn't expected was her first ever visit to the cottage when, having walked from room to room exploring, she then came to find us and announced seriously, 'You do know this place is haunted, don't you?' She was not at all perturbed by the prospect of sharing her house with a ghost – in fact, make that two ghosts.

We had allocated one of the bedrooms to be my daughter's room and had furnished it with twin beds, anticipating that she might like to bring a school friend with her on future holidays. We had also had built-in wardrobes installed and it soon became obvious that there was a problem with one of the wardrobe doors, which refused to stay shut. Time after time it would suddenly and unexpectedly swing open and, although we asked the firm who had installed the wardrobes to come back and check, they were never able to rectify the problem. Eventually we decided that it was probably caused by uneven walls or floors and resorted to putting a chair in front of the door to stop it opening. Countless times after we had been out for the day our daughter would go up to her bedroom and report that the chair had been moved while we were out and the wardrobe door was open again.

Towards the end of our first family holiday at the cottage, our daughter appeared in our bedroom in the middle of the night, complaining that there was a man in the wardrobe. Strangely, she didn't appear at all frightened by this situation but was instead rather grumpy because the man was 'hammering nails' and the noise was keeping her awake.

Artist's impression of the seated lady and the old man who appeared at the cottage in Week St Mary. (Drawings by Melanie Crawford)

Over the years, several people who slept in her bedroom reported seeing an old man wearing a leather apron, who appeared in the corner of the room apparently tapping nails into something with a small hammer. (Some people believed that he was a cobbler, mending shoes.) More worryingly, at least two people independently saw what seemed to be the same man hanging from a ceiling beam within the wardrobe, his head inclined limply to one side.

We never made any attempt to investigate the history of the house but instead just accepted our 'visitors'. As the years went on, we simply saw less and less of them, although most people visiting the cottage for the first time would report some sort of sighting at breakfast after their first night.

Within a few years, we very rarely saw anything untoward although we did occasionally hear bursts of an unidentified tapping sound, similar to the sound of a person tapping in small nails or tacks. (We reasoned that the ancient plumbing was most probably responsible for the noise.) The only strange thing that we did notice was that, on occasions, tiny piles of fine beach sand would appear on the upstairs landing.

By the 1980s, our daughter had grown into a young woman and had recently become engaged. Although she and her fiancé were not yet married, my wife and I allowed them to spend a holiday at the cottage together, when it quickly became apparent that our 'sitting tenants' did not approve of such permissive parenting.

Several times during their stay, the bedclothes were suddenly and inexplicably 'snatched' from their bed in the middle of the night. The television switched itself on

Week St Mary. (© N. Sly)

and off at will and the wardrobe door not only opened by itself but then subsequently slammed itself shut with a resounding crash, splintering the wooden plinth that separated the two doors.

However, the strangest incident occurred when my daughter and her fiancé had been out for the day to a nearby beach. When they returned home, they found that a ripe, juicy tomato had been carefully and very precisely placed on each and every tread of the staircase! The tomatoes had been in a brown paper bag in the larder when they had left earlier that day and my daughter had the only key to the cottage, with the exception of one spare key that was, at the time, several hundred miles away in the Midlands.

My daughter and her fiancé eventually married and afterwards spent many happy holidays at the cottage. Oddly enough, once they were legally married, there were no further incidents – no strange sounds, no electrical disturbances, no piles of sand on the landing, no men and women roaming around and definitely no fruit.

We eventually sold the cottage after the death of my wife in the 1990s, by which time there had been no unusual activity of any kind for about ten years.

MARCH

Dartmoor, Devon

In March 1921, Ernest H. Helby, the medical officer for Dartmoor Prison, was crossing the moor on his motorcycle. In the sidecar were two little girls, variously described in the contemporary newspaper accounts as either his daughters or the daughters of the Assistant Governor of the prison.

As the motorcycle drove along the B3212 road approaching the bridge that crosses the East Dart River, just outside Postbridge, the doctor suddenly seemed to be grappling to control the bike. He shouted to the children to jump clear, which they did. Seconds later, the bike crashed and the doctor was killed. The motorcycle had recently been serviced and was in good order and the weather conditions at the time were said to be good. There seemed to be no rational explanation for the fatal accident.

The area had a history of reported accidents dating back to 1910. Among these were bolting horses, startled by something unseen to their riders, and numerous cyclists who had unexpectedly ended up in the ditch at the roadside, all who later maintained that something or somebody seemed to have snatched the handlebars out of their hands, causing them to lose control.

A few weeks after the untimely death of Dr Helby, a coach suddenly lurched off the road at exactly the same spot. All the passengers fortunately survived the incident with relatively minor injuries but, once again, the driver stated that he had felt as if invisible hands had wrenched the steering wheel of the coach out of his hands.

On 26 August 1921, there was another accident at exactly the same spot when a motorcycle suddenly veered onto the verge. This time the rider, a young soldier, survived the incident. He subsequently stated that, as he was riding his motorcycle, a pair of large, hairy hands had covered his own and forced the bike off the road.

The story of the 'Hairy Hands of Dartmoor' was reported in the *Daily Mail* of 14 October 1921. In his article entitled 'The Unseen Hands', reporter T. Gifford recounted the series of inexplicable accidents that had occurred on the moor, all seemingly centred around one particular spot. More details were added to the account in a second article in the same newspaper three days later.

In 1924, a woman holidaying in a caravan at nearby Powder Mill awoke to see a pair of hairy hands at the caravan window. The woman had the presence of mind to make the

Princetown Prison, Dartmoor. (Author's collection)

Postbridge, Dartmoor. (Author's collection)

sign of the cross, at which the hands disappeared. However, she stated at the time that she felt that the disembodied hands were evil and that they intended to do her some harm.

On 12 September 1926, in an article entitled 'Evil Ghost of a Moor Land Road', the *Sunday Express* reported yet another accident at the same spot, again involving a motorcyclist. The rider was taken to a nearby cottage by passers-by and, when he regained consciousness, he reported having been seized and violently thrown from his motorcycle. Since then there have been several other accidents and even fatalities at the same spot.

There have, of course, been several 'rational' explanations put forward for the series of accidents and fatalities. These range from those involved having drunk a little more than was good for them at nearby pubs, to an adverse camber at the particular spot in question. From personal experience, I know that the road concerned is prone to patches of black ice, although that fact is hardly relevant to those accidents reported during the summer. It is also a road that is frequently driven far too fast, especially by visitors to the area and there are also many ponies, cattle and sheep roaming freely on the moor, which are inclined to wander out into the traffic, forcing drivers to take emergency avoiding action.

Yet none of these rational explanations satisfactorily explains the phenomena reported again and again of a pair of hairy hands that seem determined to take control of vehicles, or the unseen entity responsible for frightening horses, making them bolt or shy violently, often unseating their riders.

Lynton, Devon

When the Revd Walter Stevenson Halliday died in March 1872, he left as his legacy Glenthorne House, near Lynton, which he built around 1829. However, according to the house's current owner, Halliday is still very much in residence.

In life, Halliday was rather a reclusive man, who would often hide upstairs in his study when he didn't want to see people. Today, his presence is still evident there and also in the library, where the book-loving reverend spent much of his time. On one occasion, he apparently showed his displeasure at the placing of a small gramophone in the room by banging the library doors vigorously for a period of ten minutes.

He also apparently took a dislike to a picture hung by the current owners in a corridor, throwing it violently across the room and leaving the nail on which it had been hung still in the wall, although bent double.

In an article in *Bonham's Magazine*, Sir Christopher Ondaatje says of his ghostly visitor, 'When I'm writing, particularly late at night, the old guy is always hovering around making noise. He is a friendly ghost, however, and means no harm.'

Nancekuke Common, Cornwall

RAF Portreath first became operational at Nancekuke Common on 7 March 1941 and throughout the Second World War was utilised both as a fighter unit and for ferry

Glenthorne House, Near Lynton. (Author's collection)

operations. The last flights from Portreath were in May 1945, after which the station was reduced to 'care and maintenance' only. It became a Transport Command Briefing School and was also used as a billet for Polish Resettlement Air Corps, before being taken over by the Ministry of Supply in 1950.

From then until 1976, the site was used for chemical defence. Renamed CDE Nancekuke, it was at one time Britain's primary site for the production and storage of the nerve gas, Sarin. However, production ceased in 1956 and, from then on, Nancekuke was mainly used for more innocent purposes, such as the development and production of charcoal cloth and protective suits for use by the British Forces.

The site was taken over by the Ministry of Defence and formally re-opened as RAF Portreath in 1980.

Much of the haunting activity associated with the site and the surrounding area seems to date back to the Second World War, when several young men lost their lives in plane crashes.

A man in a Polish pilot's uniform has frequently been seen approaching a now disused hangar and walking straight through the closed doors. At the nearby village of Bridge, many of the Nissen huts used as a billet for WAAFs during the war still exist and are said to be haunted by shadowy figures, including that of an airman.

At a nearby bungalow, mysterious footsteps and opening and closing doors have heralded the appearance of a man in a blue RAF uniform who has been seen sitting in a rocking chair, smoking his pipe and gazing out to sea. Whenever anyone spoke to the man, he simply disappeared before their eyes.

North Cornwall

Although I know the real names of this couple and also the exact location of their property in North Cornwall, I have been specifically asked not to reveal them. The cottage is currently let and the couple are afraid that knowledge of the presence of a resident ghost may discourage future tenants.

'Peter' and 'Jane' bought their semi-detached cottage in a village close to the North Cornish coast in March 1986. Previously used as a holiday cottage, the property had fallen into disrepair after the death of the former owner, so the couple set about restoring it and making it habitable again.

Ghosts, it seems, are often reported during property restorations or alterations, and this was indeed the case for this particular cottage. The first sign of any unusual occurrence was the presence of three distinct and very identifiable smells. The first of these was the strong smell of oranges. What was particularly remarkable about this was that neither Peter nor Jane was particularly fond of oranges and very rarely bought them.

The second smell was described as either 'Cornish Violets' perfume or the scent of the old-fashioned sweets, known as Parma Violets. The third smell was far less pleasant, being the eye-watering stench of raw sewage. On noticing this particular smell, the couple conducted a thorough investigation of the cottage's drainage system, which was found to be in perfect working order. All three smells seemed to come and go at will and were always only noted in the living room, never anywhere else in the property.

Before long, Peter and Jane began hearing footsteps, which sounded as if someone were walking along the bare wooden floorboards of the landing, which was directly above the living room. The footsteps went the full length of the landing into the bathroom at the end, then apparently through the bathroom wall into the house next door. In conversation with their neighbours, Peter and Jane established that they too had heard unexplained footsteps walking along their upstairs landing.

Before long, Jane was afforded a clear view of the ghost who, for several months, appeared at regular intervals, briskly walking the length of the hall of the cottage. She describes the man as having a strong physical resemblance to Peter. Jane often spoke to the strange man, having caught a glimpse of him out of the corner of her eye and assumed that Peter had returned home. Oddly the ghost never appeared while Peter was in the house, although it did sometimes appear while he was working outside in the garage or garden.

Jane describes the man as being considerably shorter than Peter, roughly 5ft 6in tall and appearing very solid. He had a mane of long, curly blond hair tied back in a ponytail and was always dressed in exactly the same way, wearing a navy blue fisherman's sweater, dark trousers that were mid-calf length and flared at the bottom and light-coloured calf-length boots. He always seemed to stride very purposefully down the hall looking intently in front of him, before turning a corner into the porch at the end of the hall and apparently vanishing into thin air.

Neither Peter nor Jane was in the least perturbed by their visitor and affectionately nicknamed him 'Barnacle Bill'. There was only one occasion on which Bill gave them any trouble and that was when they decided to move house.

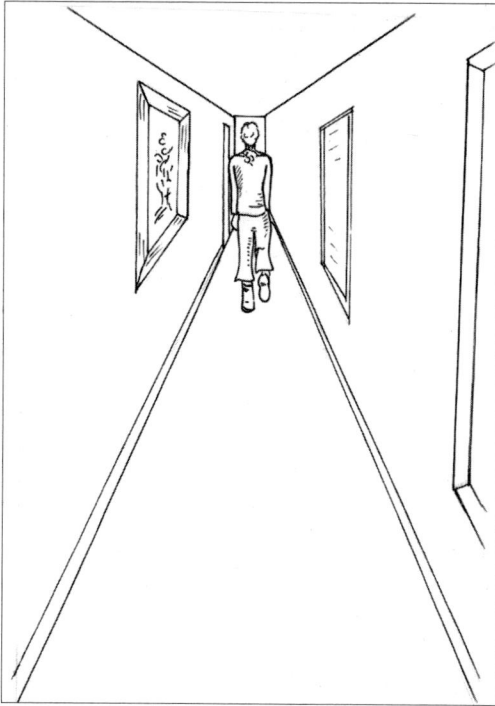

Artist's impression of the apparition that walks in the cottage in North Cornwall. (Drawing by Melanie Crawford)

Both Peter and Jane were self-employed and because of this they kept detailed accounts, which they stored carefully in a locked filing cabinet in the attic. Having found their dream property, the couple needed to obtain a mortgage, for which they had to prove their financial status. However, on going to the filing cabinet where their accounts were always kept, they discovered that the section labelled 'Accounts' was completely empty.

Both Peter and Jane had absolutely no doubts that the accounts should have been in the filing cabinet. Nevertheless they searched the entire house from top to bottom over a period of more than two weeks, returning frequently to check the filing cabinet since that was where the paperwork should have been. Finally, having had no success in locating the missing documents, they contacted their accountant who had luckily kept copies, which were quickly submitted to the building society. The mortgage application was successful and the building society returned copies of the financial papers to the couple. Much to their surprise, when they opened the drawer of the filing cabinet to replace the copies in their rightful place, they discovered the original documents carefully filed in the very section where they should have been all along, even though both Peter and Jane had thoroughly searched the cabinet several times, together and independently.

Peter and Jane moved out of the cottage in March of 1991, although they retained ownership, and the property was subsequently let to a succession of short-term tenants. Without any prior knowledge of the phenomena experienced by Peter and Jane while they were living there, many of the tenants independently reported the presence of the three strange smells, along with the sound of mysterious footsteps and a cold spot in the porch of the house where the 'man' had always vanished. As far as she is aware, Jane remains the only person to have actually seen the ghost 'in the flesh', although the couple's four cats were observed on many occasions staring fixedly as one at something or someone unseen to human eyes.

Tintagel, Cornwall

Tintagel, on the North Cornish coast, has long been associated with the legendary King Arthur and the ruined castle that stands close to the sea there is reputed to have been Arthur's Camelot.

In March 2003, Michael Fleet reported in the *Telegraph* that actress Kate Winslet had recently purchased a house in Tintagel, which came complete with its own resident ghost.

The ghost of a man, believed to have been an engineer who worked at the neighbouring Camelot Castle Hotel in life, has been seen leaving the secluded cottage in the early mornings, as if he were heading off to work.

The then joint-owner of the Camelot Castle Hotel, Mr John Mappin, is quoted in Fleet's article as saying that Ms Winslet's ghost is apparently friendly and harmless.

Camelot Castle Hotel. (Author's collection)

The old post office, Tintagel. (Author's collection)

Mr Mappin's hotel boasts three resident ghosts of its own – a nurse who wakes people up as if giving them a bed bath, a would-be art critic who has been known to throw paintings from the hotel walls if he dislikes them and another who goes through the hotel's bins, the latter evidenced by rubbish which has been observed inexplicably jumping out of them.

Ms Winslet herself is no stranger to Arthurian legend, having played Princess Sarah in the 1995 film *A Kid in King Arthur's Court*.

APRIL

Blackawton, Devon

Oldstone House at Blackawton in Devon was completely destroyed by fire in February 1895 and is now just an ivy-covered ruin. However, it was once a grand house, occupied by Martha and William Dimes and their four children.

One daughter, Laura Constantia Dimes, who was born in December 1861, was a beautiful and popular girl who loved riding to hounds. Normally her groom accompanied her when hunting, but one day she went out alone and met a young man, Hugh Rutherford Shortland.

Twenty-two-year-old Laura fell madly in love with Shortland, who, it seems, came from a good family but was involved in some rather shady business dealings in the area. Shortland, who was a year older than Laura, reciprocated her feelings and the couple made up their minds to get married.

Laura's parents did not approve, so the couple obtained a special licence and married at Kingsbridge Register Office on 8 April 1884. On that day, Laura went for her usual morning ride (presumably having sworn her groom to secrecy) and returned home a married woman.

Immediately after the wedding, Hugh had to leave to go to New Zealand, so he went straight off to make arrangements for his trip, leaving his bride to ride home alone and break the news of her marriage to her parents.

On 25 April, less than three weeks after her wedding, Laura rode out in the morning as she normally did and returned home just before midday. She changed out of her riding habit into a dress and straw hat and set off to walk her collie dog in the woods near her home. She had received a letter from Hugh that morning and, when she didn't return to the house, her parents assumed that she had gone off to meet him.

On the following morning, Laura's mother walked to Oldstone Woods, but saw no trace of her daughter or her son-in-law. In fact, it wasn't until later that day that Laura's whereabouts were finally discovered.

Elizabeth Luckcraft, the wife of one of the estate workers, was walking her own dog in the woods when she happened to glance into one of the deep ponds located there and saw the top of a woman's straw hat a few inches below the surface of the water, about 3ft from the bank. Curious, she bent down for a closer look and recoiled in horror, having seen a face and body beneath the hat. Laura Shortland was standing upright on the bottom of the pond, the water just covering the top of her hat, one arm stretched out in front of her.

The police were immediately summoned and an inquest was held a few days later at which it was pointed out that Laura's body bore no injuries whatsoever, save for a tiny, insignificant bruise on one temple. She was fully dressed, her clothing had not been disturbed in any way and there was no evidence that she had struggled or fought off an attacker. At the point where she was found, the water was just 6ft 3in deep.

It emerged that Hugh Shortland had never actually been to New Zealand but, since his wedding, unbeknown to Laura, had been staying with a friend, Mr Ryder, at nearby Modbury. Shortland and Ryder were both arrested and charged, Shortland with murder and Ryder with aiding and abetting murder, but there was not a shred of evidence against either of them and magistrates subsequently dismissed the case.

The local police then called in Scotland Yard. Laura's body was exhumed and a second post-mortem examination was carried out, but no further evidence was found.

It was indisputable that Laura had received a letter from her husband on the day of her death, although that letter was never found. Had she arranged to meet either him or Ryder in the woods? Had they argued? Did one of them strike her, causing the bruise on her temple? Was Laura pushed into the pool to drown, her feet becoming trapped in the soft, muddy bottom? Or did she commit suicide?

So many questions about the mysterious death of Laura Shortland remain unanswered. However, until the house was razed by fire, her ghost was said to regularly walk around the house and grounds and curiously, although the house was almost totally destroyed in the conflagration, the room in which Laura was most frequently seen remained relatively unscathed. The ghostly form of a woman has since been seen on numerous occasions walking through Oldstone Woods, near to the pool where Laura lost her life.

Dartmoor, Devon

In April 1929, one of the best-known characters ever associated with Dartmoor died at Llanfeachain, in Wales. David Davies, otherwise known as 'The Dartmoor Shepherd', had spent more than half of his life in jail, the longest of his many sentences having been served in Dartmoor Prison.

Davies first came to national prominence when he was 'discovered' by Home Secretary Winston Churchill in 1910. Asked to report on the success or otherwise of the 'Prevention of Crime Act', Churchill was given a list of prisoners who had been convicted as habitual criminals.

Davies was at that time incarcerated in Dartmoor. Having been found guilty of committing several rather minor burglaries, Davies had been sentenced to three years penal servitude and ten years preventive detention.

Dartmoor, 1930s. (Author's collection)

Davies was a model prisoner, described by Churchill in his report as, 'as quiet, docile and harmless a person as could be conceived.' While serving his sentence, Davies was employed as the shepherd of the Dartmoor Prison flock of sheep and was trusted to wander freely about the moor. He loved his sheep and they apparently returned the sentiment, obeying his every command and following him around like faithful puppies.

Davies had never committed any act of violence but had what Churchill described as 'an incurable mania for theft' and, by 1911, had spent twenty-eight years in prison. On the rare occasions when he had been free, he had tried to join his sister in Texas, but had been prevented from doing so both by weak lungs and by his previous criminal record, which effectively barred him from entering the USA.

Churchill ordered that Davies be released on licence. In January 1911, he was freed and was found a job as a shepherd on a farm in Wrexham, with the condition that he must work there for at least six months – he absconded two days later and, by April 1911, was in court at Oswestry charged with stealing four bottles of whisky.

Davies's name pops up in the newspapers fairly regularly until his death in April 1929, mainly in reports of local assizes, where he was frequently sentenced to further prison terms. These include a twelve-month sentence in 1913 at York for stealing 30s from a church collection box in Whitby and a three-month sentence in 1923 at Oswestry for stealing 7d from an offertory box.

Some people believe that Davies was hell-bent on getting sent back to Dartmoor where he had been so contented working as a shepherd, although it is reported that, when tried in Oswestry in 1923, he pleaded not to be sent back to prison, saying that he would rather go to the workhouse.

He finally got his wish to go the workhouse in Llanfyllin, but absconded in early April 1929 and was found dead from exhaustion and heart failure on the roadside about three miles away. His age at the time of his death is uncertain. In Churchill's original report in 1911, he was said to be sixty-seven years old, yet reports of his death in 1929 give his age as seventy-nine, while at his 1923 trial in Oswestry, he was apparently eighty-one.

Since his death, Davies' ghost has regularly been seen herding his sheep in the prison grounds and out on the moor itself. For some reason, it appears to be particularly active on misty nights.

County Ground Stadium, Exeter, Devon

I have been a speedway fan since early childhood and have accumulated a huge collection of vintage speedway programmes, which I sell to other speedway fans. When it became known that I was researching this book, several of them asked me if I planned to include the 'Exeter speedway ghost'.

A speedway team normally consists of seven riders. However, like all motor sports, speedway can be dangerous and riders are often injured. Thus a team with a member missing due to injury or illness can request the services of a guest rider, providing that the guest has a similar points average to the regular team member.

In 1962, rider Jack Unstead signed for the Exeter Falcons speedway team, transferring from his former home club, the Ipswich Witches. Sadly, Unstead was to ride just three

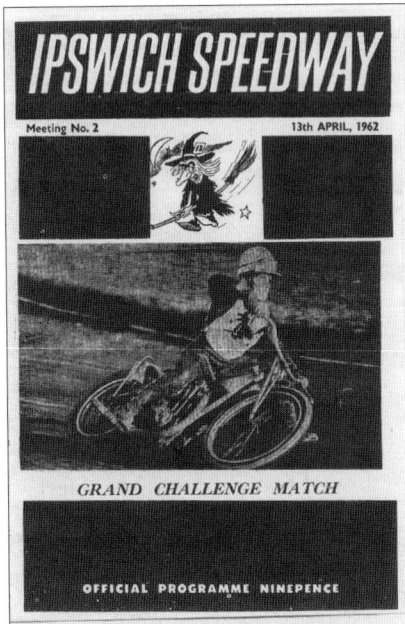

Ipswich speedway programme, 13 April 1962.
(Author's collection)

matches for his new club as, on Friday 13 April 1962, he was tragically killed while making a guest appearance at Ipswich in a home match against Southampton.

Shortly afterwards, brothers Mick and Keith – two speedway fans from Leicestershire – were on holiday in Cornwall with their families and decided to attend a speedway match at Exeter. Unsure of finding their way to an unfamiliar stadium, they set out in plenty of time, arriving at the meeting far too early.

Walking around, waiting for the stadium to open, they were surprised to see a man standing outside the gates, wearing speedway leathers. Recognising the man as Jack Unstead, they decided to ask him for his autograph. They took their eyes off him only momentarily, while they searched their bag for an autograph book and, when they looked up again, he was no longer there. Being on holiday, the men had not read any newspapers and were thus completely unaware of Unstead's tragic death.

The brothers' account was substantiated by Rod, a visiting Ipswich fan, who also told me that he believed he had 'seen' Unstead at the County Ground after his untimely death, as did three other fans and one ex-rider.

Speedway at the County Ground Stadium is sadly a thing of the past. However, at the time of writing, there are plans to resurrect Exeter speedway at a brand new track to be built at Haldon. It has been announced that a stand at the new ground will be named in honour of Unstead.

Exeter Prison, Devon

On Tuesday 6 April, thirty-three-year-old Gordon Horace Trenoweth became the last man ever to be hanged at Exeter Prison.

Trenoweth had been found guilty of the murder, on 24 December 1942, of tobacconist Albert Bateman, who ran a small shop in Commercial Chambers, Arwennack Street, Falmouth.

The Christmas period is an especially busy time for any shopkeeper, but Bateman was a creature of habit and, when he didn't return home for his evening meal, his wife went to the shop to see why he was so late. She found the doors locked and, unable to gain any response to her knocks and calls, she immediately summoned the police.

When the police broke into the shop, it was to find sixty-one-year-old Albert Bateman lying dead on the floor in a pool of blood. He had been savagely beaten and a Webley revolver had been left on the shop counter, presumably by his murderer.

The revolver was quickly traced to Plymouth docks and the police determined that the man most likely to have been in possession of it on the night of the murder was Gordon Trenoweth.

Trenoweth was well known to the police. The father of five children, his wife had been an in-patient at a mental institution since 1941 and Trenoweth had recently served a prison sentence for failing to pay for her care. Now released from prison, Trenoweth had moved in with his parents and it was at their home that he was arrested on Christmas Day.

The police were able to recover a great deal of forensic evidence that tied Trenoweth to Mr Bateman's murder. Fibres found on the revolver matched those from his jacket, an inside pocket which showed traces of gun oil. Trenoweth had two packets of cigarettes on him as well as a bank note that was positively identified as having come from Bateman's shop. Bateman had a habit of repairing any torn bank notes that he received in payment and the one in Trenoweth's possession had been mended with a piece of paper bearing Bateman's shop letterhead. Finally, bloodstains were found on Trenoweth's clothes, which were of the same blood type as the murder victim.

Trenoweth denied everything at his trial, claiming to have been looking for work at a coal yard at the time of the murder. His alibi was confirmed by the owner of the coal yard, as well as by Trenoweth's father and sister, who testified that he had returned home at 5.40 p.m. and not left home again until 6.30 p.m.

The time of Mr Bateman's death was judged to be at around 6 p.m., meaning that if Trenoweth's witnesses were to be believed, he could not have committed the murder. However, the forensic evidence, coupled with testimony from two people who stated that Trenoweth had been spending money very freely immediately after the murder, proved compelling and the jury at his trial found him guilty, albeit with a strong recommendation for mercy. The jury's recommendation was not heeded and Bateman went to the gallows.

In 1973, two long-term prisoners serving their time at Exeter Prison saw a man walking along a prison landing to a cell door, where he apparently faded away into thin air. The two men reported the sighting, but their story was initially pooh-poohed by the authorities. Yet the men persisted in their accounts of what they had seen and eventually the sighting was investigated more thoroughly. It was discovered that the cell in question was the old condemned cell and that the physical description of the mysterious vanishing man closely matched that of Gordon Trenoweth.

There are continuing reports of the sound of footsteps walking along the upper landing, even though the condemned cell has now been bricked up and completely sealed.

Lanhydrock, near Bodmin, Cornwall

Lanhydrock near Bodmin, now managed by the National Trust, is considered by many to be the finest house in Cornwall. Set in 450 acres of parkland, the house was originally a farm owned by the priory of St Petroc in Bodmin. It was bought in 1620 by Sir Richard Robartes, who immediately began building a mansion on the site. Sadly, Robartes died in 1634 without completing the project, which was then continued by his son, John.

By 1861, the estate was in the hands of John Thomas Agar-Robartes, but on 4 April 1881, the house was consumed by a devastating fire, which left only the north wing, entrance porch and gatehouse standing. Lady Juliana Agar-Robartes, aged sixty-eight, was rescued by ladder from an upstairs window, but sadly died in hospital from shock a few days later.

Lanhydrock House, 1960s. (Author's collection)

The house, which was taken over by the National Trust in 1953, has been completely rebuilt since the fire. In addition to the property, the National Trust also acquired several ghosts, one of which is said to be that of Lady Agar-Robartes. Staff and visitors to the property have also reported hearing the sound of a child giggling and the noise of heavy furniture being moved. In addition, the ghost of a man hanged at Lanhydrock during the Civil War has been said to walk the estate.

Okehampton, Devon

Now a luxury hotel, Lewtrenchard Manor was once the home of the Gould family, the most famous descendant of which was the Revd Sabine Baring-Gould, who in addition to writing many of our best-loved hymns, including Onward Christian Soldiers, was also a prolific writer of both fiction and non-fiction books throughout his life.

In 1766, Margaret Gould was left a widow with two children, Edward and Margaret. Edward grew up to be an inveterate gambler and, it was rumoured, a murderer, who died at an early age. By the time of his death, he had gambled away much of the estate and his mother Margaret set about recovering it.

Always a strong-willed woman, she was known as 'Madam Gould'. Even during her final illness, she refused to take to her bed and died in her favourite armchair on 19 April 1795.

At the very moment of her death, it is said that all of the house shutters flew open spontaneously and that a farmhand rushed to the house to investigate the commotion. Even as he stood in the room with Madam Gould's dead body, he happened to glance out of the window and saw the old lady standing beneath a walnut tree in the garden, as large as life.

Above: *Lewtrenchard.*
(Author's collection)

Left: *The Gould family tomb, Lewtrenchard.*
(© N. Sly)

A few days later, a man saw Madam Gould sitting in a ploughed field. He raised his hand in greeting and she waved back. Having just returned from America, the man was unaware of the old lady's death, until he mentioned their meeting to his family.

Since then, the figure of Madam Gould, dressed from head to foot in a white gown, has regularly been seen in the area surrounding Lewtrenchard Manor. It is said that she once confronted a little girl who had stolen some apples from the orchard and demanded that the child empty her pockets. In 1832, she is said to have risen from her grave and pursued a carpenter who opened the Gould family vault in the local churchyard.

Her activities had not ceased by the time her great-great grandson, Sabine Baring-Gould, inherited the house in 1872. Footsteps still echoed across the upper floor and a visitor to the house believed that he had seen the ghostly figures of a woman and a wigged man sitting on either side of the drawing room fireplace, where Margaret Gould customarily sat with her friend, Parson Elford. At a ball thrown by

The grave of Sabine Baring-Gould, Lewtrenchard.
(© N. Sly)

Baring-Gould in honour of his daughter's coming of age, several guests remarked on the presence of a woman standing at the edge of the room, pointing out her incredible likeness to a portrait of Margaret Gould hanging on the wall. In 1918, two nurses who were looking after Baring-Gould's grandchildren handed in their notice after seeing the figure of a woman bending over the children's beds.

More recently, guests at the hotel have apparently commented on unexplained cold spots and there have been reports that a cradle on a landing has been observed rocking without human assistance. A woman in white has been seen walking down the stairs and it is thought that the spirits of both Sabine Baring-Gould and his father, Edward, also visit the property. On occasions, children's laughter has been heard in the house and gardens.

Penfound Manor, Poundstock, near Bude, Cornwall

During the English Civil War of 1642-1646, Cornwall remained a Royalist stronghold, yet there were still some staunch Parliamentarians throughout the county, one of whom was John Trebarfoot of Poundstock, near Bude.

Trebarfoot fell in love with Kate Penfound, whose father, Arthur, was a staunch Royalist. Although there had been marriages between the two families in the past, now the hatred between the two warring factions was such that a marriage between the young lovers could never have been countenanced. Hence they made the fateful decision to elope.

The date of their planned elopement was 26 April, probably in 1643, although the actual year is the subject of much debate and has been placed as late as 1650. John raised a ladder to Kate's bedroom window at midnight. She climbed down, but Kate's father caught the couple before they could flee into the night. He ran at John with a sword and a ferocious fight ensued between the two men.

John was stabbed and died almost instantly. Arthur accidentally stabbed Kate, who had tried to come between her sweetheart and her father to stop them from fighting. She later died from her injuries, as did Arthur who had been badly wounded in the fight.

Above & below: *Two views of Penfound Manor. (Author's collection)*

PENFOUND MANOR, NEAR BUDE

The Trebarfoot family memorial, Poundstock Church. (© N. Sly)

Kate's ghost is said to haunt the manor, particularly the staircase and the room that used to be her bedroom. Every year, on the anniversary of the battle, the ghosts of John Trebarfoot and Arthur Penfound are said to re-enact the duel between the two men in the courtyard.

Roughtor, Cornwall

The moorland of Roughtor was the site of one of Cornwall's most infamous murders, that of servant girl Charlotte Dymond in 1844. For some years, Charlotte had been courting Matthew Weekes, a fellow servant at her workplace, Penhale Farm near Davidstow. However, she became involved in a flirtation with another servant, Thomas Prout, which sent Matthew almost mad with jealousy.

Roughtor. (© N. Sly)

Charlotte Dymond's grave, Davidstow. (© N. Sly)

The memorial to Charlotte Dymond, Roughtor. (© N. Sly)

On 14 April 1844, Charlotte left Penhale Farm, never to return. Her body was found several days later lying close to a small stream at Roughtor, her throat slashed from ear to ear.

Several people had seen Matthew Weekes, who walked with a pronounced limp, walking on the moor with Charlotte on the day she disappeared. Weekes was tried for the murder of his sweetheart, found guilty and executed at Bodmin Gaol on 12 August 1844.

The site of Charlotte's murder is today commemorated by a large granite monument, which marks the spot where her body was found. Here there have been numerous sightings of the ghost of Charlotte Dymond, particularly on or around the anniversary of her death. She is described as wearing a long gown, a red silk shawl and a bonnet, exactly as she was dressed when she walked out onto the moor for the last time. Among the many people who have witnessed the apparition of the young woman tramping the moor were members of the Callington 5th Corps Cornwall Rifle Volunteers, who also reported seeing mysterious lights while on night duty on Roughtor.

MAY

Bodmin, Cornwall

On 8 May 2001, the *Cornish Guardian* published an article, written by Nikki Sargeson, which was a plea for help and information from the owner of the Maple Leaf Café in Bodmin. Fiona Thompson told reporters of what seemed to be the regular appearance of a male ghost at the café, usually at around four o'clock in the afternoon.

The front door of the café was often heard to open and close on its own. During the previous summer, both the owner and a waitress had clearly seen a man walking upstairs. However, when they went up to take his order there was nobody there, even though anyone leaving the upstairs room would have had to walk downstairs again and could not possibly have done so without passing the proprietor and waitress. On occasions, the man was said to stand by the till, watching workers in the kitchen, and staff and customers have also heard strange coughing noises.

The newspaper brought in a psychic medium, who claimed to have made contact with a previous tenant of the premises. According to the medium, the man and his brother had both served with the Duke of Cornwall Light Infantry during the First World War. The brother had died in the conflict and the supposed male presence at the café had been wounded. He had returned to Bodmin and begun a relationship with his brother's widow, but their romance had ended.

Fiona Thompson assured the *Cornish Guardian* journalists that the ghost did not appear to be evil, although she and the staff found being alone in the café 'quite spooky'.

Devonport, Plymouth, Devon

On 31 May 2004, the *Plymouth Herald* reported on the findings of a team of paranormal investigators who had been called in by the Royal Navy to try and solve some of the unexplained phenomena reported at the Naval Base at Devonport.

The focus of the investigations were the Hangman's Cell, which houses what is thought to be the last remaining functional gallows in Britain, and the Master Rope Maker's House, which dates back to the eighteenth century and has previously been described as the most haunted place in Plymouth.

Devonport, Plymouth. (Author's collection)

The Royal Naval Barracks, Devonport, 1914. (Author's collection)

It is believed that more than 140 French prisoners of war were executed at Devonport during the Napoleonic Wars and base personnel have variously reported sightings of: a young girl dressed in Victorian costume, a sailor, a woman in a long gown, an eighteenth-century naval officer, a little girl playing with a doll, and a bearded man who was frequently heard humming tunes. In addition, there have been reports of unexplained cold spots and sudden drops in temperature and of lights being inexplicably switched on when there was nobody present. On occasions, a man's face appears, looking out of the window of a supposedly empty attic.

People have reported being pushed and furniture has been moved. Windows appear to open and close by themselves and, as well as the humming sailor, footsteps, banging noises and even the sound of a horse-drawn carriage have been heard in the vicinity. One family, who lived in the Master Rope Maker's House in the 1970s, claimed that the Formica work surfaces in their kitchen were once completely torn to pieces.

At the end of their weekend investigation, the team stated that they believed 'beyond any degree of doubt' that they had detected paranormal activity at the base.

Four years later, in August 2008, the *Daily Mail* published an account from a cleaner who had seen a mysterious sailor dressed in an old-fashioned trench coat, carrying a duffle bag slung over one shoulder. The man appeared so solid that the cleaner actually spoke to him, bidding him 'Good morning'. The man smiled at her, at which the cleaner briefly turned away. When she looked back moments later, the man had completely disappeared.

His only possible exit, without walking straight past the cleaner, was through heavy glass doors but, according to the cleaner, the doors were extremely noisy and, had the man opened them, she would definitely have heard him.

Kenton, near Exeter, Devon

On 9 May 1855, the *Manchester Guardian* printed an article in which it was claimed that the inhabitants of the village of Kenton, which lies just outside Exeter, had been terrorised by the presence of a ghost.

An unnamed inhabitant of the village had died while away from home and, before her death, had requested that her body was buried in the churchyard at her native village. However, her dying request was not granted and, not only that, but her money passed to one of her daughters, to the exclusion of her other children.

These circumstances combined were, according to the villagers, sufficient to ensure that the old woman's spirit would never rest in peace and shortly after her death, lights were reported moving around in her empty cottage, usually at around ten o'clock in the evening, when it had been the old lady's custom to retire to bed.

People flocked from surrounding villages at the appointed time every night to watch the mysterious lights flickering from room to room in the darkened cottage.

Eventually, the village schoolmaster, Mr Jones, decided to spend a night at the cottage and professed himself to be quite untroubled by any ghost throughout his solitary vigil. This divided the opinions of the villagers, some of whom were reassured and others who continued to believe that the spirit of the old lady had returned to her home, even though her physical body had not.

Lapford, Devon

On 23 May 1861, the Revd John Arundel Radford was buried at Lapford Church, where he had been the incumbent vicar for many years.

There is anecdotal evidence that 'Parson Jack', as he was known to his parishioners, murdered his curate, but he was acquitted because the jury said that they had never yet hung a man of the cloth and weren't about to start. While I have not been able to verify the murder, there is abundant evidence that John Radford's behaviour during his incumbency at Lapford was most unbecoming for a man of his status.

Throughout the 1850s, there are numerous reports of him being summoned for failure to pay his bills and a further account of a trial for poaching, at which he was found guilty and given a fine. In December 1851, he took out the following notice in the *Exeter Flying Post*:

Notice – To Shopkeepers, Tradesmen and Others Whereas Thomasin Elizabeth Radford, my Wife, has contracted Debts without my knowledge (after having been repeatedly requested not to do so) thereby causing me great vexation and trouble, and heaping on me insuperable difficulties, I therefore hereby warn and give Notice to all persons whomsoever, not to harbour or trust the said Thomasin Elizabeth Radford, or any of my family, as I will not be answerable for, or pay any Debt or Debts that either she or they may in future contract. John A Radford Dated Lapford, December 10th, 1851.

By February of the following year, he was again in court, summoned by a local butcher who was seeking settlement of an outstanding debt of £39 12s 3d for meat. However unhappy his marriage to his wife Thomasin might have been, a report of the incident in *The Times* states that the couple had thirteen children together!

His repeated court appearances for bad debt continued until, in January 1855, he was charged at the Chulmleigh Petty Sessions with assaulting a constable. A bailiff had visited Radford to serve a summons on him for yet another outstanding account. The bailiff had taken the precaution of asking a parish constable to accompany him and Radford had struck the constable four times then forcibly ejected him from his premises.

Found guilty by the magistrates and ordered to pay a fine of £4 5s, including costs, Radford vowed that he wouldn't pay a farthing and was promptly sent to Exeter Prison for one month.

Having served his sentence, Radford returned to Lapford where he resumed his clerical duties. Described in *The Times* as 'a powerful, athletic man' who had for many years been addicted to field sports and displayed an 'extraordinary bluntness of manner and conversation', John Radford survived only another six years, dying at the age of sixty-two.

Lapford. (Author's collection)

Lapford. (Author's collection)

In life, John Radford had always expressed a wish to be buried in the chancel of the church where he had served for so long as rector, threatening to come back and haunt his parishioners if his request were denied. In the event, he was buried outside the vestry door, a position which he was obviously unhappy about, as he has allegedly haunted the village ever since. Legend has it that Radford decreed that his headstone would never stand straight if he was buried anywhere other than his chosen location – however, a visit to Lapford Church will confirm that few, if any, of the headstones there are straight.

Sampford Peverell, Devon

John Chave and his family, along with their servants and William Taylor (who was Mrs Chave's brother) occupied a huckster's shop in Higher Town, Sampford Peverell. Prior to Mr Chave's tenancy of the property, it seems that there had been a solitary report of a sighting of the ghost of a woman at the house, made by an apprentice, which nobody had taken seriously. However, when the Chave family took up residence apparent poltergeist activity began in earnest with a serious of thunderous knockings and raps that appeared to emanate from the upper floors.

By May 1810, the activity had escalated to the extent that the female servants were being physically attacked nightly, being beaten by unseen fists. At least three of the servants appeared to sustain an actual injury at the hands of the unseen entity and it was noted that, if there were no women present in the house, or if the women were asleep, the paranormal activity ceased. The fearsome noises echoing throughout the house intensified until they were almost constant. They included the sound of footsteps walking downstairs and continuing through a solid wall. Curtains were rattled ferociously and a sword and a Bible were thrown violently through the air. On one occasion, Mr Taylor saw the sword suspended in mid-air pointing directly at him, although it subsequently fell harmlessly to the floor.

A strange monster was seen roaming about the property, compared by one witness to an enormous black rabbit, which fled when approached, disappearing through the close-set palings of the garden fence.

The local clergyman, Revd Caleb Colton, was called to investigate and later wrote an account of the apparent paranormal activity in a pamphlet entitled 'Plain and Authentic Narrative of the Sampford Ghost'.

The story was picked up by the *Taunton Courier*, whose reporting of the affair was largely disbelieving in tone. The authenticity of the ghost had divided the residents of Sampford Peverell, many of whom suspected that John Chave had deliberately faked the paranormal activity in an effort to purchase the property at a greatly reduced price. Revd Colton sprang to Chave's defence, pointing out that at no time had he shown any interest in buying the property. Some villagers believed that Chave was involved in smuggling or other illegal activities and had created the stories of haunting in order to frighten people away from the property. However, others were convinced of the

Higher Town, Sampford Peverell, 1917. (Author's collection)

existence of the Sampford ghost; one anonymous person was so certain of the truth of the facts that he sent a death threat to the newspaper's editor in protest at the apparent cynicism expressed by his paper.

On 18 August 1810, the *Taunton Courier* published a letter from Caleb Colton, in which he swore an oath that he had spent four nights at the property, and had seen and heard the phenomena for himself and that he was unable to attribute the various activities he had witnessed to any human hand.

During the course of his investigations, he had personally sealed every single door and cavity in the house, through which any communication could be carried on, with a wax seal applied to each end of pieces of paper in such a way that the slightest attempt to open such doors, or to pass such cavities, would have broken these papers. Not one seal had been disturbed.

Several women not connected to the family in any way had spent a night at the house and, without exception, each had reported a disturbed night punctuated by repeated blows, the opening and closing of curtains, pressure from a suffocating weight on their bodies and infernal noises, which, on occasions, were sufficiently loud to cause the room to shake.

All of these women were willing to be interviewed and to swear an oath to the authenticity of their experiences, as were more than twenty other reliable and trustworthy people, some of whose names Colton listed at the end of his letter:

Mr. JOHN GOVETT, Surgeon, Tiverton
Mr. BETTY, Surgeon, Tiverton

Mr. PULLING, Merchant, Tiverton
Mr. QUICK, Landlord of the White Horse, Tiverton
Mr. MERSON, Surgeon, Sampford Peverell
JOHN COWLING, Esq., Sampford Peverell
Mr. CHAVE, Mere, near Huntsham

In September 1810, the case made the national newspapers and on 18 October, *The Times* printed a deposition from John Govett, the Mayor of Tiverton. The deposition was dated Thursday 27 September 1810 and was a sworn statement from John Chave, William Taylor and servants Sally Case and James Dodge, made before Govett in his official capacity as mayor.

It stated that they were all completely ignorant of the cause of all the extraordinary occurrences at Chave's house and that none of them had personally ever made any of the noises or struck any of the blows or indeed made any attempt whatsoever to trick anyone into believing that there was supernatural activity afoot and neither had they requested anyone else to do so on their behalf. Furthermore, each of the four stated that if anyone else was responsible for perpetrating a hoax, it was without his or her knowledge or consent.

The four swore before Govett that they were all anxious and eager to discover the cause of the phenomena. They attested that marks observed on the walls and ceilings of the property were the result of investigators trying without success to replicate the noisy disturbances in the house in order to produce a rational explanation. Furthermore, to their knowledge, there were no subterranean passages in or about the house.

Revd Colton pointed out to the newspapers that if the Sampford ghost were a hoax then its perpetration now involved at least fifty people, who were all willing to perjure themselves on oath to claim their innocence of any trickery or fraud. Eventually Colton offered a reward of £250 to anyone who could solve the mystery and, although that sum equated to a small fortune in the early 1800s, the reward was never claimed.

Tywardreath, Cornwall

On an inside wall of the parish church at Tywardreath is a plaque commemorating the former MP for Fowey, William Rashleigh and his wife Caroline. Rashleigh died on 14 May 1855 and strange occurrences have been reported inside the church on the anniversary of his death.

A plume of black 'smoke' has been seen issuing from the memorial tablet and forming itself into a shape said to be human. The figure then drifts around the church before dispersing, often accompanied by loud banging noises and, in 1997, by the crash of a wall hanging falling from the wall onto the floor.

At other times, one of the church bells is said to ring without the assistance of any human hand and a former cleaner has reported seeing the figure of a monk standing in the aisle. The apparition quickly 'dissolved' as she looked at it.

JUNE

Barnfield House, Exeter, Devon

Henrietta Marie was born in Paris in November of 1609, the youngest daughter of King Henri IV of France. At the age of fifteen she married Charles, Prince of Wales, their marriage requiring a special dispensation from the Pope, since she was a Catholic and he a Protestant.

The difference in their religions alarmed the English Parliament and, when Charles was crowned King Charles I in February 1626, Henrietta Marie was not allowed to be crowned beside him.

At first, the marriage seemed to be more a union of convenience than a love match, but gradually the couple became devoted to each other. In 1642, with a Civil War looming in England, Henrietta Marie fled to the Netherlands. However, she returned to England and the king in February 1643 and was soon pregnant with her ninth child.

She went to the relative safety of Bath for her confinement but was forced to move even further west to Exeter as the Parliamentarian army, led by the Earl of Essex, advanced into the South West. On the 16 June 1644, the queen gave birth to a daughter, Henriette Anne, at Barnfield House in Exeter.

On 14 July 1644, the queen left Falmouth for France. Her beloved husband, Charles, was executed in January 1649 and, from that moment onwards Henrietta Marie went into mourning.

Her ghost, dressed in black, is said to walk the gardens of Barnfield House to this day.

Castle an Dinas, Cornwall

Castle an Dinas is one of the largest ancient hill forts in the county of Cornwall. Excavations of the area have indicated that it was used mainly during the Iron Age, although some evidence has been found of a Neolithic causeway, suggesting an even earlier origin. It has long been associated with legends of King Arthur and is said to be the place where Cador, Duke of Cornwall, and King Arthur's mother, Ygraine, were killed. In the twentieth century it became the site of a Wolfram mine. Given its ancient history, it is perhaps not surprising that the area is said to be haunted.

Kenegie Manor, which is now a hotel, 1962. (Author's collection)

One legend linked to the site is that of 'Wild Harris', who lived at nearby Kenegie Manor. Harris was enamoured with a young woman, a distant relation who had fallen on hard times and had thus moved into the manor house. Entirely dependent on the charity of her relatives, the young woman was like a fish out of water at the manor, being considered too low to associate with the family and yet too high for the servants. She was particularly despised by the old housekeeper, a spiteful, malicious woman who ruled the house with a rod of iron. The housekeeper saw the girl as a threat, fearing that she might marry Wild Harris, the son of the household. The housekeeper spied on the clandestine meetings between the two young lovers and reported back to Harris's father, who would have much preferred his son to marry someone more in keeping with his status as future lord of the manor rather than an impoverished orphan. The squire threatened that, if his son married their poor relation, he would marry his housekeeper to prevent his son from inheriting the Kenegie estate.

So great was the opposition to the marriage of the young lovers that the orphan girl fell into a state of depression and sadness and eventually left the house one night under the cover of darkness. Her body was found the following morning, drowned in a nearby millpond.

With his sweetheart gone, Harris devoted himself to his other great love: hunting. In due course, the old squire died, finally giving his son the satisfaction of turning the spiteful old housekeeper out of the house. However, so bitter was the old lady at her treatment that she fretted herself to death and soon returned to haunt her old domain, making such a noise about the house that its inhabitants had no peace.

Night after night she would shriek and scream, rattle plates or beat the furniture, keeping the occupants of the house awake until her footsteps were heard going up the stairs and along the gallery to her master's bedroom, when the nightly din finally ceased. Her shadowy figure, dressed in a long gown, was often seen passing through the courtyard outside the house and she was not above aiming a vicious slap or a kick at young servant girls. It is said that her restless and noisy spirit was eventually confined to a small room in the manor house containing a fleece from a black sheep. She was set the impossible task of carding the fleece over and over again until it became white then spinning it into stockings. The entrance to her room was boarded up with only a tiny hole left in an outside wall. Legend has it that if the hole was ever blocked, it was reopened almost immediately by unearthly means.

Wild Harris spent his days hunting and his nights revelling with friends. Yet he too came to an untimely end while still in the prime of his life. Whilst out hunting at Castle an Dinas one day he was thrown from his horse and killed. The animal was said to have been startled by a white hare, which was believed to have been the spirit of the woman he had loved and lost.

It was customary at the time to hold funerals at midnight and Wild Harris's body was taken to Gulval Church and buried in the churchyard there. When the mourners returned to Kenegie for the wake, they were greeted by the ghost of Wild Harris standing by the summerhouse in the garden. He was dressed in his hunting clothes and his faithful hound was at his feet. (The dog had been so attached to Harris that it had simply lay down and died when his master drew his last breath.)

For many years, local people were reluctant to pass the old manor house in the dark, for fear of hearing the sounds of Wild Harris carousing with his friends. Eventually the Revd Mr Polkinghorne of St Ives, a renowned exorcist of the time, was called in to rid the manor of evil spirits. He succeeded in banishing Wild Harris's ghost to the

Gulval Church. (Author's collection)

Castle an Dinas. (Author's collection)

summit of Castle an Dinas, where it was given the task of counting the blades of grass nine times.

While the account of Wild Harris is a Cornish legend, the facts behind the tragic murder of eighteen-year-old Jessie Rickard at Castle an Dinas in June 1904 are more easily verifiable. Jessie was the sweetheart of a local carpenter, twenty-year-old Charles Berryman, who was almost obsessive in his love for her. The couple went for a cycle ride to Castle an Dinas where, having heard that Jessie was interested in another man, Berryman fired six shots at the young woman, five hitting her in the face and neck and the sixth entering her elbow.

Jessie died instantly and Berryman later turned the gun on himself, dying from a bullet wound to his head. A photograph of Jessie was found in his pocket along with a letter to his mother giving instructions on the disposal of his effects.

The reports of ghosts at Castle an Dinas are many and varied. There have been sightings of ghostly armies and people have reported hearing the sounds of phantom battles. Gunshots have also been heard and many people have found themselves suffering from dizziness or unexplained trembling at the summit, some reporting intense pains in the head.

St Nectan's Glen, Cornwall and Hartland, Devon

There are numerous legends surrounding St Nectan. Believed to be the oldest son of the Welsh King Brychan, born around AD 468, Nectan left Wales and sailed to the West Country, landing at Hartland on the North Devon coast, where he built a church and a hermitage. Today, several churches in the area bear his name and the supposed date of his death – 7 June – is commemorated by services.

Around AD 500, Nectan is believed to have moved from Devon to Cornwall, establishing a retreat at St Nectan's Glen or Kieve, near Tintagel. (Kieve being the Cornish word for basin.)

St Nectan's Kieve.
(Author's collection)

St Nectan's Church, Stoke, near Hartland. (Author's collection)

There are several differing accounts of his death, the most frequently quoted being that he was given a cow by a local farmer after he had helped him by rounding up the farmer's pigs. Robbers determined to steal the cow and, in the resulting skirmish, Nectan was beheaded. He allegedly surprised his killers by picking up his severed head and walking back to his retreat with it.

Nectan is said to have had a silver bell, which he rang to warn the villagers at Tintagel when ships were in danger off the treacherous Cornish coasts. Shortly before his death, he supposedly threw the bell into the water at the Kieve, vowing that it would never again ring for unbelievers. It is rumoured that the sound of the bell is still heard on stormy nights.

After Nectan's death, two women, thought to have been his sisters, claimed his body, burying it in an oak coffin beneath the stream that runs through St Nectan's Glen. The two women continued to live in the hermitage until they too died and were buried by villagers under a large, flat stone.

The area is reputed to be haunted by St Nectan and the two women, whose ghostly forms have often been seen walking through St Nectan's Glen, as have the hooded figures of monks. People also speak of hearing the strange sounds of sobbing, laughter, monastic chanting and even organ music echoing through the valley on the approach to the Kieve.

At St Nectan's Church at Stoke, near Hartland, witnesses have seen the figure of a monk, both in the church and in the churchyard. These witnesses include the vicar, who saw the monk on two occasions during the 1970s. The area near Hartland Abbey is also said to be haunted by a procession of monks dressed in long, brown or black habits, while two headless ladies have been spotted at nearby Bow Bridge. Many of those who have seen the women state that they have been able to hear the rustling of their silk dresses.

St Nectan's Glen. (Author's collection)

Stoke village, near Hartland. (Author's collection)

Sennen, Cornwall

Throughout the nineteenth century, much of the Cornish coastline was a perilous place for shipping due to the prevalence of smugglers, who would risk life and limb to dishonestly obtain the ships' precious cargoes of tobacco, spirits, silk, tea and other highly prized commodities. On 5 June 1805, thirty-five-year-old John George of Sennen paid the ultimate price for his smuggling activities, being hung at Newgate Prison, having been found guilty of the crime of inciting a riot.

George had been tried at the Old Bailey on 24 April 1805, charged that he and others:

> … being armed with fire-arms, guns, pistols, pikes, swords, and large stones, unlawfully did assemble themselves together, aiding, abetting, assisting, rescuing, and taking away from William Parry, an officer of our Lord the King, a thousand gallons of brandy, rum, and geneva, and five hundred pounds weight of tobacco, being respectively uncustomed goods, after the seizure of the said goods.

The principal witness for the prosecution was John George's sister-in-law, Anne, the wife of his brother Joseph.

According to evidence given at the trial by William Parry, he had been forewarned by Anne and Joseph George that the smugglers intended to attack him and to reclaim the contraband that he had just seized. Soon there was a pitched battle being fought between around thirty villagers and the revenue men, during which several of Parry's men were seriously injured in a prolonged barrage of musket fire and stone throwing. According to Parry, Anne and Joseph George tried several times to negotiate with the smugglers on his behalf and, had it not been for their efforts, the seized goods would surely have been lost.

John George was infuriated by his brother's actions and vowed that since Joseph 'was gone like a rogue to inform the officers' he would 'shoot him as soon as he would shoot a black-bird.'

Anne's apparent treachery against her brother-in-law was not the first time that she had crossed the smugglers of the village. It was said that she and Joseph were landlords of the First and Last Inn at Sennen and that they occupied the premises rent free due to their intimate knowledge of the activities of the inn's owner, Dionysius Williams. When Williams tried to evict them, Anne turned King's Evidence against him, resulting in his imprisonment. She had also supposedly given evidence at the trials of other village smugglers.

Legend has it that the villagers of Sennen swore revenge on Anne George for standing witness against her brother-in-law and that when she returned to the village she was horribly murdered by being staked on the beach at low tide and covered with fishing nets. As the tide rose, she was drowned.

Once the tide had receded again, Anne George's body was taken back to the First and Last Inn, where it was laid out in one of the first-floor bedrooms, before being

First and Last Inn, Sennen, 1950s. (Author's collection)

buried in an unmarked grave in the cemetery next door to the pub. Even though long dead, it seems as though Anne still wishes to lay claim to the bedroom at the inn that once was hers.

People sleeping there are said to have suffered from terrible nightmares, in which they dreamed that they were drowning or experience the sensation of being pinned to the bed, unable to move. Often people say that they found it difficult to breathe.

Doors slam unexpectedly and previously locked windows are inexplicably found wide open. Parts of the pub suddenly go very cold and people walking on the upstairs landing have reported feeling as if they are being watched or followed, and several people have said that they felt that they had been touched by an unseen hand.

The figure of an old woman dressed in black has been seen standing at the side of the bed in 'Anne's bedroom' and the pub cats have been found shut inside closed cupboards and drawers.

JULY

Buckfastleigh, Devon

The legends surrounding Richard Cabell, who was once the squire of Buckfastleigh, are numerous. He is reputed to have murdered his wife, although that particular legend can be reliably discounted, since his wife lived on for several years after his recorded death on 5 July 1677.

Cabell's remains are interred in the churchyard of Holy Trinity Church at Buckfastleigh and, on the night of his burial, it is said that he rose from death to lead a pack of phantom hounds across the surrounding countryside, continuing his lifelong love of hunting from beyond the grave. Every year, on the anniversary of his death, Cabell was said to rise again to lead the hounds, who first bayed frantically at his graveside, impatient for him to appear.

Rumoured to have sold his soul to the Devil, Cabell was said to have been a monstrously evil man in life. In an effort to lay his soul to rest, a fortress-like tomb was built around his grave, protected by iron bars, and an enormous slab was placed on top of his grave to prevent its occupant escaping. Even so, there have been reports of a strange, red light emanating from within the tomb and of a host of demonic figures prowling around the grave, trying to obtain Squire Cabell's soul for their master. Local legend states that anyone who runs around the grave seven times, then sticks their hand through the iron bars will get their fingers bitten, either by Cabell or by the Devil himself!

There are a series of natural caves beneath the church at Buckfastleigh and in these caves a combined stalagmite and stalactite have formed into a shape known locally as 'Little Man'. Little Man resembles a man dressed in seventeenth-century costume and is alleged to be located directly beneath the grave of Squire Cabell.

Other reputed sightings of the ghost of Squire Cabell are of him seated in a coach driven through the country lanes around Buckfastleigh at breakneck speed, the vehicle pulled by headless horses and driven by a headless coachman.

The church where Cabell is buried is an isolated one and, in the nineteenth century, the graveyard was frequently targeted by body snatchers, driven by the willingness of the doctors of the time to pay handsomely for human cadavers for anatomisation. It is easy to theorise that the legends surrounding Squire Cabell may have arisen from

The ruins of Holy Trinity Church, Buckfastleigh. (© N. Sly)

Left: *Richard Cabell's tomb, Buckfastleigh. (© N. Sly)*

Below: *Holy Trinity Church, Buckfastleigh, 1960s. (Author's collection)*

a need to protect the church and graveyard – after all, what could be a better deterrent to anyone intending to visit a graveyard at night than the suggestion of the presence of a malevolent ghost and a pack of hellhounds?

That said, the church has certainly experienced more than its fair share of disasters. The tower was struck by lightning in the 1880s and there have been two serious arson attacks, the first in 1849 and the second on 21 July 1992, which left the church completely gutted, leaving just a bare shell still standing. Many people blamed the arson attacks on Satanists, although this has never been substantiated.

The legend of Squire Cabell is also said to have been the inspiration for Sir Arthur Conan Doyle's book *The Hound of the Baskervilles*. Conan Doyle apparently visited the area and was told a version of the legend – the coachman who drove him around during his visit was a Mr Baskerville.

Bude, Cornwall

Soon after Mary's aunt died on 17 July 2000, Mary was surprised to receive a telephone call from her cousin to say that the old lady had left her a specific piece of jewellery in her will. A few days later, a parcel arrived at Mary's home near Bude and, when she opened it, she was delighted to find that her legacy was a solid gold locket and chain, obviously an antique.

The heart-shaped locket had a surface of dark blue enamel on both back and front, each overlaid with a pattern of gold. Hinged on one side, the locket opened to reveal an elaborate knot of human hair in one half and three engraved initials in the other.

The hair was very fine and pale blonde in colour and the first of the three initials was impossible to read, although the second and third were quite clearly the letters A and F, written in italic capital letters. The only strange thing about the locket was that it had a most unusual smell, which Mary would later describe as being 'sharp and vinegary'.

Bude, Cornwall, 1950s. (Author's collection)

Bude, Cornwall. (Author's collection)

It happened that Mary was due to celebrate a milestone birthday and she felt that the locket would complement her new outfit. She noticed that, while wearing it, unlike most metal jewellery, the locket didn't seem to warm in contact with her skin, but remained ice cold. However, Mary didn't wear the locket for too long that evening as, on her way to the restaurant – while still completely sober – she tripped and broke a bone in her foot.

The break was a bad one and Mary spent most of the night in the Accident and Emergency department of the Cottage Hospital at Stratton. Several months later, when the bone still hadn't healed properly, it was decided that Mary needed to have one of her toes amputated.

The locket lay almost forgotten in Mary's jewellery box for nearly two years, when Mary decided to wear it for yet another trip to a restaurant. Once again, she was struck by the locket's strange smell and by its coldness against her skin.

This time, the meal passed without incident. However, the following morning, Mary received a telephone call to tell her that, shortly after leaving the restaurant, the friend she had been dining with had suffered an unexpected heart attack. Luckily, he survived.

On returning from the restaurant, Mary had undressed for bed and placed the locket on her bedside table. When she awoke, she found the locket in bed with her and, over the next few days, she noticed that wherever the locket was placed in her house it would invariably move, sometimes into a completely different room.

The locket is now kept securely in a safety deposit box in a Bude bank and while Mary allowed me to photograph it, she was very keen to ensure that it was safely back

The Victorian locket. (© N. Sly)

under lock and key as quickly as possible. Having done some research into the locket, Mary believes that it is a piece of Victorian mourning jewellery and that whoever it commemorates is not happy for the locket to be worn by a person who didn't know him or her in life. Having handled the locket, I can confirm Mary's account of a strange, almost acidic smell and that the locket seemed icy cold, even after having been clutched in my closed hand for several minutes. (By that time, Mary's almost palpable nervousness and her insistence that the locket had, over the years, 'absorbed fear' didn't seem at all fanciful.)

Whether Mary's aunt ever experienced any similar accidents is not known. However, Mary does have in her possession a photograph of her late aunt and uncle, taken on the day before her uncle's death. The picture clearly shows that Mary's aunt is wearing the locket around her neck.

Exeter Cathedral, Devon

At seven o'clock in the evening during the month of July, the ghost of a nun is said to glide along the south wall of the nave of Exeter Cathedral, vanishing quickly as soon as she is seen.

She joins a phantom monk, a three-headed entity who walks the Cathedral Green, the ghost of a past caretaker who haunts one of the chapels, and a tall, gaunt ghost who, in the 1940s, is supposed to have frightened two men who were engaged in stealing lead from the roof of a nearby building.

Exeter Cathedral. (Author's collection)

Off Padstow, Cornwall

During the First World War, the Germans made extensive use of U–Boats to try and cut essential supplies to Great Britain by destroying both military vessels and merchant ships. Convinced that this was the way to break the British and so win the war, Germany produced more and more of the sinister U–Boats, one of which was the infamous UB65.

The contract to build UB65 was awarded to Vulcan AG in Hamburg in May 1916 and the 'Iron Coffin' as it was nicknamed immediately proved to be somewhat cursed. Within the first week of her construction a giant girder, which was suspended by chains over her hull, suddenly plummeted to the ground, trapping one worker underneath. His workmates struggled to free him for more than an hour but, just as they finally succeeded in lifting the huge beam, the man died. A subsequent enquiry could find no fault with the chains and failed to find any rational explanation as to why the girder should have fallen.

A second tragedy marred the construction of UB65. Inexplicably, while workers were testing the dry cell batteries in the ship's engine room, the batteries began leaking toxic fumes and three workers were overcome. All three men died before they could be rescued.

In spite of these problems, UB65 was successfully launched into open seas for testing. Before long, a sailor was swept overboard and drowned when the submarine surfaced. The captain immediately ordered the boat to dive but, as it did, a ballast tank sprang a leak and the engine room was flooded. Once more the batteries began to

A German U-Boat, 1910s. (Author's collection)

emit toxic fumes, although thankfully the submarine managed to surface without any further loss of life.

The UB65 went back to port for repairs but as she was being armed for active service, a torpedo exploded, killing the second officer and injuring several other members of the crew. The officer was buried with full military honours and the crew were given a few days of shore leave while the boat was made seaworthy again.

However, just as UB65 was about to be re-launched one of the members of the crew approached the captain in a state of panic, having seen the dead second officer boarding the boat. The captain was naturally sceptical until a second crew member approached him and independently recounted seeing the second officer walking purposefully up the gangplank to the bow of the boat where he stood gazing out to sea for a few moments before simply disappearing before the sailor's eyes.

News of the ghostly presence of the deceased second officer spread like wildfire among the crew of thirty-four men and, perhaps unsurprisingly, there were yet more sightings. The captain tried his best to quell the stories, doubtless fearing an outbreak of mass panic and hysteria, but by January 1918, he could no longer dismiss the accounts as being the product of overactive imaginations.

The UB65 was patrolling the English Channel, off Portland Bill, when a heavy storm broke out. The captain ordered the submarine to surface and, as soon as it had reached the surface, he stationed a lookout on the deck. To his amazement, the lookout suddenly became aware of a man standing nearby. Thinking the man foolhardy to be on deck in such appalling weather, the lookout was about to shout a warning when he realised that, with the sole exception of the hatch he himself had just climbed through, the remainder of the UB65's hatches were firmly battened down. There was no way that the man could have climbed out through the hatch used by the lookout without walking past him to get to the position he now occupied. The lookout took a closer look at the man on deck and realised to his horror that it was the deceased second officer.

He immediately rushed down below, screaming to his shipmates that the dead officer's ghost was on deck. Realising that he had to stem the tide of panic that was rapidly rising below deck, the exasperated captain scrambled quickly up the ladder and flung open the hatch. There, as the lookout had reported, stood a man, his face distorted but still recognisable as that of the deceased second officer. After a few moments, the apparition faded away and vanished.

The UB65 returned to Germany where high-ranking officers interviewed each of the crew independently. As one, each swore that he had been sharing the submarine with a ghost.

The crew were eventually dispersed and deployed on other vessels, while the UB65 was sent to Belgium, where a Lutheran minister was called upon to exorcise it. It was then redeployed into service with a new captain, Martin Schelle, and a completely different crew. By May 1918, the sightings of the ghost officer had begun again.

A petty officer swore that he had watched the dead officer walk through a solid bulkhead into the engine room. A torpedo handler became so distressed at receiving nightly visits from the dead man that he eventually threw himself overboard and was drowned.

The ultimate fate of the UB65 is disputed. She is recorded as being lost by accidental cause (marine casualty) off Padstow, on or after 14 July 1918. However, a slightly conflicting account of her eventual destruction tells of an American submarine, which spotted the surfaced UB65 on 10 July 1918. As the American submariners were loading torpedoes in readiness to fire at her, the UB65 suddenly exploded and then sank with the loss of all hands.

The wreck of UB65 lies on the seabed about six miles from Padstow, at a depth of approximately 60m. Researched by the Channel 4 television programme *Wreck Detectives* in 2004, their divers describe the submarine as being 'relatively intact' and saw no evidence of any explosion having occurred, although the hatches were all found to be open, suggesting that the crew had made some attempt to escape.

South Petherwin, Cornwall

In the year 1665, a terrible epidemic spread though the town of Launceston, killing several of its residents. One of the unfortunate victims was John Eliot of Trebursey, who was just sixteen years old.

John's funeral was held on 20 June 1665, conducted by the Revd John Ruddle, who also ran Launceston Grammar School, the school that Eliot had attended before his untimely death. As Ruddle left the church after the service, he was approached by the concerned parents of another young boy, Stephen Bligh.

According to Mr and Mrs Bligh, their son had become depressed and surly of late and was very reluctant to go to school. Everyone had tried their hardest to find an explanation for the sudden change in the boy, suggesting that he was either lazy or that he had fallen in love. Apparently Stephen's only explanation for his behaviour was that he was being haunted by an evil spirit on his daily journeys to and from school at South Petherwin.

As requested, Ruddle went to visit Stephen at his home and the two had a candid heart-to-heart talk. Stephen assured Ruddle that he was not lazy but loved to study and desperately wanted to be educated. Neither was he smitten by a girl. His problem stemmed from his daily walk to and from school, which regularly took him through a field on Botathen Farm, known as the Higher Broom Quartils.

Neither his parents not his school friends would believe his regular encounters with the mysterious spirit, who he knew to be a woman called Dorothy Dinglet. Dorothy had died in the late 1650s. Some accounts say that she was cruelly murdered and that her killer was never brought to justice, others suggest that the unfortunate woman died in childbirth, the father of the baby being Stephen Bligh's older brother. However she died, it seemed that Dorothy Dinglet did not rest easy in her grave. A tall young woman in her early twenties, with a pale complexion and light brown hair, Dorothy regularly passed by Stephen Bligh, gliding rather than walking along the farm footpath, never looking at him, never speaking and never responding when the boy tried to speak to her.

Stephen's change in character was the result of sheer frustration at not being believed, coupled with fear of the apparition that was not only appearing before him with increasing regularity but was also beginning to haunt his mind, occupying his every waking moment and tormenting his dreams. In desperation, he had changed his route to school, taking Under Horse Road rather than the footpath across the fields. However, the apparition also took a new route and Stephen would now regularly meet Dorothy in the narrow lane between the Quarry Park and the nursery.

To placate the boy, Ruddle offered to go with him to the spot where he had most frequently met Dorothy Dinglet and the two rose early on the following morning, when Stephen directed Ruddle to a field in open country, about three furlongs from the nearest dwelling. Sure enough, the ghost of Dorothy Dinglet appeared in the field and was clearly witnessed by the Revd Ruddle.

Ruddle had pressing business to attend to that took him away from the area for a few days but, before he left, he promised Stephen that he would return, which he did on 27 July 1665. On that morning, Ruddle walked the footpath alone and, just as she had when he was accompanied by Stephen a week or so earlier, Dorothy Dinglet suddenly appeared out of nowhere and walked swiftly across the field about 30yds away to his right.

Ruddle went straight to the Bligh's home and spoke to Stephen's parents, suggesting that they should all go to the field together on the following morning to see if the apparition would reappear.

To the absolute horror of the Blighs, who had known Dorothy Dinglet well before her death and had even attended her funeral, the apparition appeared before them that morning, climbing over a stile and gliding swiftly across the field before disappearing over a second stile. Ruddle and Stephen Bligh immediately gave chase, quickly reaching the stile that Dorothy had just climbed over. The two stood on a hedge bank and peered over into the next field, but there was absolutely no trace of Dorothy. According to Ruddle's subsequent written account of the sighting, 'even the fastest horse in the country could not have run so fast as to be out of sight in that short space of time.' Meanwhile, a spaniel dog that had accompanied the party on their quest to see Dorothy Dinglet, had barked frantically at the strange apparition, before turning tail and fleeing home as fast as it could.

The Blighs quickly followed their dog, vowing never to walk the footpath again. However Ruddle was made of sterner stuff and was determined to communicate with the apparition if that were possible.

Accordingly, he rose early on the following morning, 31 July, and went to the field alone, spending an hour or so in quiet meditation and prayer. Once again Dorothy Dinglet made an appearance and, this time, when Ruddle spoke to her, she was persuaded to come closer to him and eventually to speak, although in a voice that was barely audible and largely unintelligible.

Having successfully communicated with Dorothy Dinglet, Ruddle left the field, returning later that evening when he once again initiated a conversation of sorts with the apparition. This time Ruddle was successful in persuading the ghost to leave and from that moment on Dorothy Dinglet was never seen again.

Ruddle faithfully recorded his exorcism of the ghost of Dorothy Dinglet in an article, dated 4 September 1665, which was passed down through his family. It was first published in 1720 in Mr Campbell's *Pacquet for the Entertainment of Ladies and Gentlemen*.

The legend of Dorothy Dinglet persisted at least until the beginning of the twentieth century, when threats of her appearance were used to frighten young farm labourers, who had to walk the lonely footpath on their way to their work.

Note: As might be expected in an account of this age, there are some variations of names and spellings in various different tales of the ghost of Dorothy Dinglet. Her name is alternatively given as Dingle, Dinglet and Dinglett, while the Revd Ruddle's name is also spelled Rudall. The farm at which Miss Dinglet regularly appeared before Stephen Bligh is referred to as Botatan or Botathen and the particular field where her presence was most often observed is called both Higher Broom Quartils and Higher Brown Quartils.

AUGUST

Ludgvan, Cornwall

Sarah Polgrean had endured a hard life. When she was only four months old, her father was killed in an accident. Her mother was unable to cope with raising her daughter alone and consequently abandoned her to the care of the parish at Gulval, near Penzance. Sarah received little formal schooling before being apprenticed into service at the age of nine and, during her apprenticeship, it seems certain that she was sexually abused by at least one of her fellow servants.

When she left service, Sarah took to roaming the country, never staying in one place for too long. Eventually she met and married a soldier who took her to London, but the couple soon realised that their marriage had been a mistake and parted by mutual consent, after which Sarah returned to Cornwall, the county of her birth.

In due course, she met and married her second husband, Henry Polgrean. Yet, once again, her marriage was far from happy, mainly because Sarah continued to be free with her sexual favours. Understandably, Henry grew jealous and the couple had frequent, often violent rows about her promiscuity.

A particular favourite of Sarah's was a man known as 'Yorkshire Jack', who is variously described as either a horse dealer or a sailor. It appears that Jack truly captured Sarah's heart as, possibly with his encouragement, she set out to free herself from the shackles of marriage by poisoning her husband.

Henry fell ill on 14 July 1820 and died soon afterwards. Although his death was initially thought to be due to natural causes, villagers immediately placed the blame for his demise on Sarah. The buzz of gossip about her reached such a pitch that the police were no longer able to ignore the allegations and decided to exhume Henry Polgrean's body just eleven days after its burial. When the contents of his stomach were analysed, they were found to contain large amounts of arsenic.

It was noted that Sarah had recently purchased arsenic from a shop in Penzance, saying that she needed it to kill rats at home. Yet the house that she had shared with her husband had never been known to have a problem with vermin. Hence Sarah was arrested and charged with the wilful murder of her husband. At her trial at Bodmin in August 1820, she vehemently denied any involvement in her husband's death, but to no avail. The jury found her guilty of murder and she was sentenced to hang.

Bodmin Gaol, the site of the execution of Sarah Polgrean. (© Kim Van der Kiste)

Sarah did eventually make a full confession to the murder of her husband and went to the gallows on 12 August. She made just one request, which was that Yorkshire Jack should be allowed to walk with her to the scaffold.

The couple were allowed a final kiss and there was an exchange of whispered words between them. When the executioner indicated that it was time for them to part, Sarah looked directly into Jack's eyes and solemnly asked, 'You will?'

'I will,' replied Jack.

Almost from the moment of Sarah's death, Jack became a changed man. It was, people said, as if he were haunted. He lost weight and grew pale and haggard. He eventually confided to the villagers of Ludgvan that he had promised Sarah on the scaffold that, living or dead, he would become her husband in three years time and now Sarah was trying to ensure that he kept his promise from beyond the grave.

With the agreed time for his 'marriage' fast approaching, Jack fled to sea in an effort to escape the demands of his would-be bride. However, as his ship returned from a trip to the Mediterranean bearing a load of fruit, there was a terrible storm. Fellow sailors reported hearing the ringing of distant wedding bells as the storm raged, but Jack would not willingly go to his bride. Finally, a huge wave washed him overboard from the deck – Sarah had finally got her man.

During storms, sailors in Mount's Bay have often reported hearing the unexpected sound of wedding bells and a disembodied voice saying, 'I will, I will …'. And Sarah herself has been sighted in the churchyard at Ludgvan, where several members of the

Polgrean family are buried. The apparition wears a long, white shroud and bears the faint trace of a mark of the hangman's rope around her neck.

Morwenstow, Cornwall

One of the most famous former residents of Cornwall was Robert Stephen Hawker, known to all and sundry simply as 'Parson Hawker'. His father served as the vicar of Stratton and Robert himself became a minister, initially serving as a curate in North Tamerton. In 1834 he became the vicar of Morwenstow, a position he held until his eventual death in August 1875. Hawker was an eccentric man, rather rotund in stature and favouring bright coloured clothes over the more traditional black clerical garb. He was a great lover of animals and, in addition to a pony and nine cats, he kept a pet pig, Gyp, which followed him around like a well trained dog.

On his arrival at Morwenstow, he found the vicarage in a state of disrepair and immediately set about designing and building the large imposing house that still stands there today. He added numerous personal touches to the building, including chimneys modelled on the towers of the four churches at which he had served and a kitchen chimney that replicated his mother's tomb.

Hawker was known both for his impulsive generosity and for his artistic temperament. He wrote several hymns and poems during his lifetime, including the

Parson Hawker. (Author's collection)

Morwenstow Church. (Author's collection)

Cornish anthem 'The Song of the Western Men'. Much of his composing was done in a small hut on the cliff tops at Morwenstow, which he fashioned himself from driftwood. Twice married, his first wife, Charlotte, died in 1863. In 1864 he married Pauline, a Polish lady whom he had met when she visited Cornwall in her capacity as governess to the children of a family from Yorkshire.

Towards the end of his life, Hawker experienced a deep depression coupled with feelings of paranoia and persecution. He became an opium smoker in an effort to ease his troubled mind but the drug merely exacerbated his mental problems. As he approached his death, he began to have leanings towards the Roman Catholic faith and on his deathbed he was received into the Catholic Church. This conversion caused considerable controversy, as people immediately questioned his loyalty to the Anglican Church, which he had faithfully served for all of his working life.

Hawker's first wife, Charlotte, is buried within Morwenstow Church, directly in front of the pulpit. It had always been Hawker's intention to be buried near to her, but his wish was denied and he was eventually buried in Ford Park Cemetery in Plymouth. His tombstone bears the inscription 'in the Catholic faith', words which would undoubtedly have prevented his interment in the churchyard by the sea that he so loved.

The ghost of Parson Hawker has been observed standing in the churchyard, ruefully surveying the place where he wished to be buried. His plump figure in its rather garish clothes has also frequently been seen walking the lanes in the area, always heading for the church.

His driftwood hut on the cliffs has the distinction of being the smallest property owned by the National Trust. Visitors to the hut have commented on the occasional

The Bush Inn, Morwenstow. (Author's collection)

Hawker's hut. (Author's collection)

smell of pipe smoke, tinged with a strange sweetness such as that created by Hawker's opium. In spite of the stunning views of the beautiful but rugged Cornish coastline that can be seen from the hut, many people find that they suddenly become unaccountably depressed when they enter, describing the atmosphere as oppressive and terrifying, while others claim to experience feelings of euphoria.

One of Hawker's actions in life was to assist in trying to rescue sailors whose ships were wrecked on the treacherous rocks at Morwenstow. He felt it was important to give those men who didn't survive a Christian burial, even if, as was frequently the case, their identities could not be established. He buried the remains of more than fifty sailors in the churchyard, including all but one of the crew of the sailing ship *Caledonia*, which ran aground in September 1842. There were just two survivors of the wreck, one a sailor and the other a tortoise, which was quickly adopted by a local boy.

The ship's figurehead, personally retrieved by Parson Hawker, marks the grave of the captain of the *Caledonia* (it was restored in 2008). The figurehead, which depicts a man in traditional Scottish costume, his sword raised as if in attack, has attracted a number of superstitions over the years, the main one being that if anyone walks thirteen times around the figurehead in an anti-clockwise direction the ghosts of the dead sailors will rise up as one.

The Lost Gardens of Heligan, Near Pentewan, Cornwall

At the beginning of the nineteenth century, the house and grounds at Heligan were inherited by Henry Hawkins Tremayne, a curate from Lostwithiel. Tremayne had a grand plan for the gardens at Heligan and his son, grandson and great-grandson – all of whom became horticulturists – followed in his footsteps and devoted themselves to improving the gardens.

Between them, they introduced many foreign plants such as tree ferns and palms and created a kitchen garden capable of supplying the house with not only fruit and vegetables but also more exotic fare such as pineapples, citrus fruits, grapes and melons. A large number of gardeners were needed to tend the eighty-acre gardens and the estate employed many young men from the area. In August 1914, one of them scrawled a message on the lime-washed inside wall of a garden toilet that read 'Don't come here to sleep or slumber', beneath which many of the estate's young gardeners signed their names. Some of the names have faded over time but those still visible almost 100 years later read: W. Durnsford, W. Guy, R. Barron, ? Carhart, C. Dyer, C. Ball, D. Hocking, ? Paynter, ? Paynter, ? Paynter, Albert Rowe, W. Rose, Vercoe, Vickery and L. Warne.

Sadly, many of the names are repeated on the war memorial in nearby St Ewe. With the outbreak of the First World War, most of the workforce was sent to fight in France and the majority never returned. The very heart had gone out of the gardens, which were simply abandoned to nature. The great house became a convalescent home for soldiers and later a billet for American soldiers during the Second World War. It was divided into flats during the 1970s.

During the 1990s, the gardens were gradually restored to their former glory, a project that continues to this day. However, the work appeared to disturb several of the property's ghosts, many of which Tim Smit describes in his book *The Lost Gardens of Heligan*.

There have been reports of doors opening and closing and of footsteps echoing through the corridors of the flats. In a part of the gardens historically known as 'Grey Lady's Walk', the apparition of a woman dressed in grey has been seen walking away from the house, while a ghostly form appears to vanish through the solid wall of the Crystal Grotto.

In 1978, an Australian plumber was engaged to carry out some work on the house and decided to camp out in the then overgrown Melon House. Having collected together a few sticks, he attempted to light a fire, but the wood stubbornly refused to catch light. After repeated attempts, he had almost given up when the fire suddenly burst into flames, which shot skywards in the unmistakeable form of a cross before the fire died completely, leaving only a small pile of cold ashes.

A more recent event occurred in the Melon House when the lids of forcing pots were observed being systematically lifted in turn, as if by an unseen hand. The head gardener complained that seeds were being moved, even in locked rooms, and another member of staff reported seeing a huge black shape appearing out of the ground in broad daylight, before it drifted off and vanished. Whatever the shape was, it was also apparently seen by the man's dog, which unaccountably stood frozen to the spot with her hackles raised, refusing to approach the area where the shape was observed.

Eventually the local vicar was asked to visit the gardens and, after consultation with the bishop, a simple ceremony was performed at each of the allegedly haunted sites, since when the ghostly activities have apparently ceased.

However, numerous visitors to the gardens have spoken of feeling as if the spirits of their lost loved ones accompanied them, while others have described feeling as though they were not alone.

Personally, I have made two visits to the Lost Gardens of Heligan and am full of admiration for the project. Yet, while I have never considered myself as being particularly sensitive to 'atmospheres', the gardens at Heligan are one of only two places where I have persistently felt as though I was being watched. (The other location was at the site of an ancient gibbet in Somerset.)

I have also spoken to a man who firmly believes that he encountered a ghost at Heligan. He was walking towards the areas known as the Jungle and the Lost Valley, with his normally sedate Labrador ambling contentedly beside him on a lead, when the dog suddenly snatched the lead from the man's hand and disappeared into the undergrowth, barking excitedly.

Knowing that his dog should not be loose, the man immediately set off in pursuit, luckily catching the dog before it had progressed too far off the path. As he grabbed the lead, the man looked up to see a man standing in the undergrowth a few yards away, wagging his finger in disapproval.

The dog's owner raised his hand in apology and turned back to the path. He had only taken about two or three steps when it struck him that the man had been dressed in a very old-fashioned style. While he was obviously wearing 'working' clothes, these included a collar and tie and a flat cap. The dog owner turned round for a second look, but even though he had clearly seen the man just seconds earlier, there was nobody there.

Penzance, Cornwall

On 11 August 1845, Benjamin Ellison was hanged for a terrible murder, which was committed at Rosevean Road in Penzance on 7 July of that year. It was described in *The Times* on 14 July as, 'one of the most appalling murders which it has ever fallen to our lot to record.'

At that time, Ellison, aged sixty-one, had been living as man and wife with Elisabeth Ruth Seaman for around eighteen months. However, on the night of 7 July, he called at the Temperance Hotel in Prince's Street for some refreshment and asked if he might stay there for the night, as it was too late for him to go home.

He was given a bed and stayed until between five and six o'clock the following morning, when he left the hotel and went to the home of a Mrs Mary Hill, his next-door neighbour in Rosevean Road.

He told Mrs Hill that his house had been broken into and Mrs Seaman murdered. Mrs Hill went with him to the property, where she was met with a sight that *The Times* reported as 'horrifying in the extreme.'

Elisabeth Seaman lay on the floor in a pool of blood, her face covered by a black gauze veil and her head almost completely severed from her body. A large, bloodstained hatchet was found on the floor, near to where her body lay. The back of her head had been smashed like an eggshell and other parts of her body were 'dreadfully cut and mangled'. Having shown Mrs Hill the body, Ellison announced his intention of going to fetch a magistrate.

On the day of the murder, there was great excitement at Penzance, as the first stones for the new pier and the new market house had been laid. Most of the inhabitants had flocked to witness the celebrations, thus it was hardly surprising that no sounds of any argument had been heard from the cottage at Rosevean Road. Indeed, Ellison himself had attended the events, calling on a neighbour to accompany him and saying that Elisabeth Seaman was too busy to do so. However, later that evening, one neighbour, Elizabeth Richards, had been walking home from the festivities when she heard what she described as 'fearful, dreadful, horrid groans' coming from Ellison's house. She had been too frightened to stop and investigate further.

Ellison's own hands were very bruised, his face was covered with fresh scratches and one of his thumbs appeared to have been bitten. He had been seen by neighbours walking towards the house at about seven o'clock on the evening before the discovery of Mrs Seaman's body and, most damningly, the dead woman was clutching a fistful of hair, identical in colour to Ellison's.

Ellison's false teeth were found in the grate in the room where Elisabeth Seaman lay dead and a bundle of clothes, similar to garments he had been seen wearing in the past, were found stuffed in a cesspool close to the beach. There were numerous valuable items in the house, yet nothing appeared to have been stolen and, shortly before the murder, Benjamin and Elisabeth had both made wills, each naming the other as the main beneficiary.

When Benjamin Ellison was tried before Mr Justice Erle at the Bodmin Assizes, less than a fortnight later, it took the jury just ten minutes of deliberation to find him

Penzance, 1950s. (Author's collection)

guilty of the wilful murder. Asked if he would like to address the court, Ellison made a lengthy speech declaring his innocence and accusing the witnesses of telling lies against him. However, it was later reported in the contemporary newspapers that he had written a letter to a Penzance resident in which he had confessed to being the murderer.

After the murder, the house on Rosevean Road stood empty for some time before it was next inhabited. Since then, many residents have claimed that there is an overwhelming feeling of great sadness and despair within its walls, a sensation which was so oppressive and all-pervading that several occupants have declared themselves unable to stay in the house because of it.

In addition, the sound of heavy footsteps is regularly heard echoing from the street outside the cottage, particularly late at night. The footsteps seem to walk down the middle of the road, often ceasing abruptly outside the murder cottage. Anyone who hears the footsteps and happens to look out of a window invariably sees an empty street. People walking along the street at night also claim to have heard the footsteps following them and have immediately turned round to see nobody behind them. For many years, local people believed that they were the footsteps of Benjamin Ellison, returning to the cottage to claim his next victim.

SEPTEMBER

Chambercombe Manor, near Ilfracombe, Devon

On 26 September 2006, Living TV aired an episode of *Most Haunted* in which their team of investigators visited Chambercombe Manor near Ilfracombe. The manor is believed to date back to the eleventh century and was mentioned in the Domesday Book. Although now more of a farmhouse than the grand manor it once was, it was owned by distant relatives of Lady Jane Grey and she is known to have stayed at the property.

The house is steeped in legend, the main one concerning the discovery of a hidden room in 1865. The story goes that the then owner was carrying out some renovations on the house and, while repairing the roof, discovered the outline of a window. As there was no known room in which the window could have been located, the owner eventually broke through the wall of the bedroom where Lady Jane Grey once slept and found an adjoining chamber that had been completely sealed. Inside the chamber was an ornate bedstead and on the bed was the skeleton of what was later found to be a young woman.

There are many stories surrounding the identity of the mysterious young woman, but perhaps the most persistent is that she was the daughter of a former owner of the house, William Oatway.

William was the son of Alexander Oatway, a legendary wrecker who used lights to lure ships onto the rocks before murdering their crews and plundering the ships' contents. William eventually married a Spanish woman, saved from one of his father's wrecking expeditions. He brought his bride to Chambercombe Manor but, to his eternal regret, he was only able to lease the property and could not afford to purchase it outright.

In due course, the Oatways had a daughter, Katherine, who grew up to be a beautiful young woman. Kate eventually fell in love with an Irishman, who was the captain of a pirate ship and whose name is variously given as Wallis or Wallace. When the couple married, they decided to settle in Dublin and Kate left Chambercombe to sail to Ireland with her new husband, promising to return one day to visit her parents.

Some years later, there was a terrible storm on the North Devon coast and William Oatway walked down to the shore at Ilfracombe to see if there were any ships in distress. Standing on the beach at the height of the storm, William heard a faint groan and, on closer investigation, found a young woman, whose face had been damaged beyond all recognition, having been dashed against rocks by the fierce waves.

The woman was carried to Chambercombe, where William and his wife tried desperately to save her life. However, she was too badly injured and died on the following morning.

Searching her body for any clue to her identity, William found that the woman was wearing a money belt, which was crammed with enough gold coins and jewels for him to be able to achieve his long-held ambition of purchasing Chambercombe Manor.

It was only when a shipping agent called at Chambercombe Manor to ask the Oatways about a female passenger who had been reported missing from a wrecked ship that they learned the dead woman's true identity and realised that they had witnessed the death of their own daughter. Knowing that he would be forced to return the money if he admitted to the presence of the dead woman in his house, William chose instead to keep the money and concealed the young woman's body in a room that he subsequently sealed.

The spirit of Kate Wallace is said to remain at Chambercombe Manor, where strange unexplained footsteps have since been heard, in addition to a low moaning noise emanating from the chamber where her body lay. An ethereal lady in a long white dress has been seen walking in the grounds and there have also been sightings of two little girls in the upstairs bedrooms, along with unexplained poltergeist activity.

A staircase is said to have an oppressive atmosphere and there are a number of unexplained cold spots throughout the house.

One of the highlights of the *Most Haunted* investigation at Chambercombe Manor was the filming of a child's crib, apparently rocking backwards and forwards without human assistance.

Godolphin House, near Helston, Cornwall

Godolphin House near Helston was built in the fifteenth century as the seat of the Godolphin family, whose considerable wealth came from the Cornish tin mining industry. It was to this house that Sidney Godolphin brought his bride on 16 May 1675.

Margaret Blagge, who had served at court as a Maid of Honour to the Duchess of York, supposedly had an almost pathological fear of childbirth and, just three years after her wedding, her fears sadly became reality when she died from a fever on 9 September 1678, six days after giving birth to her son, Francis.

Margaret was buried in the church at nearby Breage and her ghost is said to haunt Godolphin House, particularly on the anniversary of her funeral. A 'white lady' has been seen to emerge from a sealed closet in the entrance hall of the house and then walk out onto the terrace and into an avenue of old trees. Several people, including the eminent Cornish historian Dr A.L. Rowse, have reported hearing the unmistakeable

Godolphin House. (Author's collection)

An exterior view of Breage Church. (Author's collection)

An interior view of Breage Church.
(Author's collection)

rustling of a lady's silk dress in the house and there have also been sightings of her funeral possession proceeding along what has come to be known as 'Ghost Path' en route from the house to the church.

Another member of the Godolphin family is also said to have returned as a ghost, this time in the neighbouring county of Devon. During the English Civil War, a body of Royalist soldiers stopped overnight at Chagford in Devon. As they prepared to leave early on the morning of 8 February 1643, they were surprised by a group of Parliamentarians and an impromptu battle ensued.

Among the Parliamentarian forces was thirty-three-year-old Sydney Godolphin, the then MP for Helston. Sydney was known as a gentle, peaceable man who showed considerable talent as a poet. He was simply not cut out for the realities of warfare and accounts of the skirmish suggest that he took a musket ball just above his knee and quickly bled to death.

His ghost, resplendent in its Cavalier uniform, is said to haunt the Three Crowns Hotel at Chagford to this day, appearing mainly in the porch where he fell mortally wounded, but having also been sighted in most of the other rooms.

*The Three Crowns
Hotel, Chagford.
(Author's collection)*

Penzance, Cornwall

The *Western Morning News* of 19 September 2003 carries the intriguing account of strange goings-on at the Co-Operative store at Queen's Square in Penzance.

The upstairs warehouse at the shop is said to be haunted by the ghost of an elderly lady and staff have apparently heard mysterious footsteps going up and down the stairs leading to the warehouse and have noticed that the lift doors are prone to opening and closing at will. The shop's duty manager has even come face to face with the old lady.

The newspaper story of September 2003 was prompted by a series of incidents that occurred over many months, always after the store had closed. In addition to the mysterious footsteps, staff had been troubled by unexplained power cuts and items of stock being moved overnight.

When closing the tills one evening, the three members of staff remaining in the store noticed that some cans of lager had spilled on the floor some distance away from the shelf on which they should have been stacked. When they examined CCTV footage taken of the area, it appeared to show a ghostly hand reaching out and pushing the cans off the shelf onto the floor. (The CCTV film was subsequently sent to GMTV and featured on their morning news programme.)

A local medium was called in to the store to give her impressions and spoke of feeling the strong presence of a man in the shop, who felt that he needed to 'have some fun'. However, paranormal researchers in the area remained unconvinced by the footage, pointing out that there seems to be one second missing from the film's timing, even though the filming was constant up until the moment that the beer left the shelf. While not completely dismissing the ghostly presence, they stressed the need to do more detailed research into the haunted shop.

The staff members at the store were completely unfazed by their ghostly companion, who they affectionately nicknamed 'George'.

Reel Cinema, Plymouth, Devon

Since first opening its doors on 15 July 1938, the Royal Cinema at Derry's Cross, Plymouth has undergone many transformations, including several changes of name. Now known as the Reel Cinema, the news of its impending closure in 2008 came as a shock to many local residents, who had grown up not only watching films there but also attending live concerts at the venue, including performances by The Beatles, Cream, Deep Purple and T Rex in the 1960s and '70s.

The three-screen cinema has long had a reputation for being haunted and has been the site of numerous paranormal investigations, the final one of which was planned by Plymouth Sound Unite as a charity fundraiser on 26 September 2008, just days before the cinema was scheduled to close.

Throughout the years, there have been sightings of a woman dressed in white in Screen 2, along with a little girl and another woman who apparently has a penchant for horror films. During screenings of horror movies, the phantom woman is said to always sit in a particular seat in the front row. Patrons who have occupied that seat at other times have frequently reported feeling unwell, some to the extent of having to leave the cinema in the middle of the film.

An apparition of a man has been seen in the foyer and staff and patrons alike have reported audible phenomena throughout the building, including the sounds of violins, whispering voices and organ music. (Wilfrid Southworth, the organist who played at the opening of the cinema, was tragically drowned less than a month later, while bathing in the sea about twenty miles from Plymouth.)

There have been numerous reported incidences of people being pinched or poked and patrons have also felt strangely uneasy in the ladies' toilets, often believing that they are being watched.

Shortly after the 'final' vigil (which raised £1,600 for charity) it was announced in the *Plymouth Herald* that the cinema had been granted a reprieve, following a last minute approach by a Brixham-based company.

Redruth, Cornwall

The *West Briton* newspaper of 18 September 1846 reported:

A GHOST – A real ghost was discovered on Saturday morning last, on the premises at Sinns, Redruth, and captured with very little resistance. When taken into custody, the wily spirit tried to pass himself off for a Mr. Gordon Chadwick, a thing of flesh and blood – residing in that neighbourhood, but the capturers were satisfied that it was a real ghost they had taken, and insisted on carrying the curiosity before the Revd George Treweeke, who, being by his profession qualified to estimate the dangerous tendencies of this kind of existence, thought the requirements of the case met by an humble apology

Redruth, 1904. (Author's collection)

from the sprite, and a promise that he would, in future, abstain from taking his nocturnal recreations in that particular neighbourhood.

Winkleigh, Devon

On 23 September 1975, a deliveryman called at West Chapple Farm at Winkleigh and was met by a horrifying sight. Outside one of the barns lay two dead bodies and a third body lay in the garden, just beyond the front door of the farmhouse.

The farm had been in the Luxton family for generations and, on the death of Robert John Luxton in 1939, it was divided between his three children, Alan, Robbie and Frances.

Robert Luxton had been a puritanical and parsimonious man who had denied his daughter Frances any kind of normal life by refusing to allow her to have boyfriends. Robbie inherited his father's ways and he in turn managed to thwart Alan's wedding plans.

The three siblings lived together at the farm, with Robbie actively resisting any attempts by his brother and sister to escape. Alan joined the local Young Farmers' Club and, as a result, tried to modernise the way in which the farm was run, but Robbie stubbornly refused to allow any changes to be made, believing that the traditional methods of farming should be strictly adhered to. Eventually, Alan had a nervous breakdown and was admitted to hospital. On his return to the farm, he took to spending long periods of time alone in his room.

Winkleigh, 1920s. (Author's collection)

Meanwhile, Frances made several trips abroad with friends but always returned to the family farm. As the years passed, the Luxtons became more and more reclusive and, by 1975, it was believed that Alan had not left the farm for nearly twenty years and Frances rarely left the premises, with the exception of occasional visits to family graves at nearby Brushford churchyard.

By 1975, Robbie, Alan and Frances were respectively aged sixty-five, sixty and sixty-seven years old. The day-to-day running of the farm was becoming far too much for them to cope with, particularly as Alan's health was failing. Reluctantly, the siblings put the farm up for sale and agreed a price of £90,000, with which it was believed that the Luxtons intended to buy a modern bungalow in Crediton.

Yet, having sold the farm, the reality of leaving was more than the siblings could bear, with Frances being especially upset at the thought. 'We were born on the farm and we should die here,' she insisted. Alan was also very distressed at selling the farm and the three siblings engaged in a series of never-ending arguments about what they should or should not do.

The arguments were finally settled on 23 September, with all three Luxtons dead from shotgun wounds. At a later inquest, it was determined that Alan had shot himself, after which Robbie had shot Frances then committed suicide.

It has since been alleged that the Luxtons have never truly left the farm and that, while there have apparently been no actual sightings of their ghosts at West Chapple, there are areas of the farm that seem to harbour what one person described as 'an atmosphere of bitterness and despair'. Numerous people claim to have encountered the three siblings in the streets of Winkleigh and a woman resembling Frances has also been reported sitting on a memorial bench at nearby Brushford churchyard.

Left: *The Luxton family grave, Winkleigh churchyard. (© N. Sly)*

Below: *The memorial to Alan and Robbie Luxton, behind the family grave. (© N. Sly)*

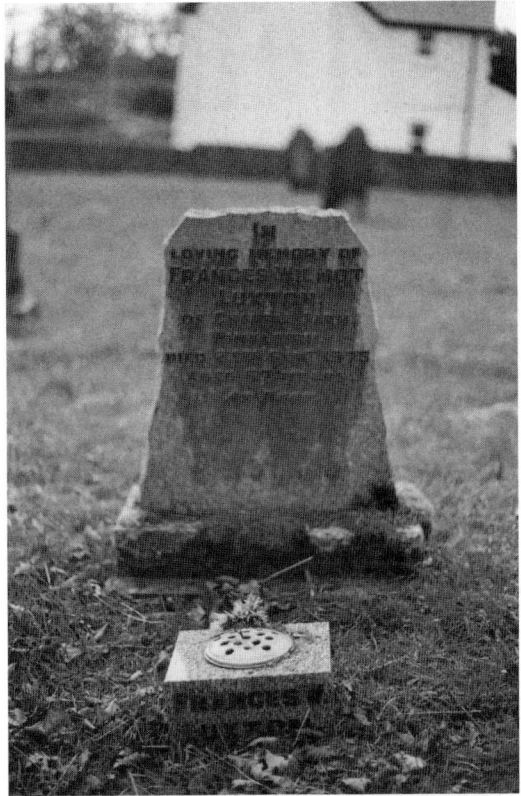

Right: *The grave of Frances Luxton. (© N. Sly)*

Below: *The memorial bench at Brushford churchyard, where the ghost of Frances Luxton is frequently seen. (© N. Sly)*

OCTOBER

Bochym, Near Mullion, Cornwall

The night of 15 October 1917 was clear and starlit and, as Sub-Lieutenant A. Jelf walked from the RNAS station at Bonython on the Lizard Peninsula to visit friends at Mullion, he could not help but notice the fragrance of the hedgerows. As he climbed the Mullion side of the Bochym Valley, deep in thought, he suddenly felt unaccountably afraid and experienced a strange compulsion to look towards a stand of trees on the right-hand side of the road. To his horror, he saw two men, who appeared to be engaged in a ferocious duel.

Although the men were about 50yds away, Jelf could see them clearly enough to describe the knee breeches, dark green cloak and pale-coloured neck ruff that the duellist on the left was wearing. The other combatant's clothing was less distinct, although Jelf recognised it as being of the same period in history.

Rooted to the spot with fear, Jelf watched as the two men fought vigorously for around a minute before one fell to the ground, apparently run through by his opponent's sword. The victor briefly bent over the fallen man, then beckoned to somebody standing in the shadows. Immediately, six men in similar dress emerged from the hedgerow, bearing a coffin, which they placed on the ground next to the dead man.

Only then did the victor seem to realise that he was being observed and turned towards Jelf with his sword arm raised, apparently frowning. Jelf promptly fainted with fear and remembered nothing else until he regained consciousness some time later. By then, all trace of the duel had disappeared, although the memory was so fresh in Jelf's mind that he ran as fast as he could to his friend's house, arriving at about 8.30 p.m., shaken and plastered with mud.

Jelf initially assumed that the entire experience was a product of 'bad digestion' or a result of the strain of his numerous flying missions from the Air Station, which served as a base for the airships used for anti-submarine sorties and observation during the First World War. Yet, as the weeks passed, he became more and more convinced that he had experienced something supernatural.

Jelf was unable to believe that a 'dream' could possibly cause him to faint, or that it could create such an enduring sense of terror, which was so acute that Jelf was

Mullion Cove. (Author's collection)

reluctant to walk the same way for many weeks after his experience. In the past, Jelf had always been extremely sceptical about any kind of psychic experience and didn't consider himself at all receptive to paranormal phenomena. He had never before felt so fearful, in spite of being in what he described as 'tight places' in the past, including active service at the Battle of Jutland. The only other possible explanation Jelf could offer for his vision was that he had somehow telepathically picked up thoughts from someone else's mind.

In April 1919, Jelf wrote an account of his experiences, some of which was later confirmed by Mr M. Kean, the man whose house he was on his way to visit. Kean described Jelf's arrival at his house on 15 October, saying that he appeared to have run most of the way and that he was covered in mud and appeared very shaken. (Both letters are currently housed at The Royal Institute in Cornwall.)

Some years later, Cornish historian A.S. Oates related a chance meeting with a vicar on a train, during which the vicar mentioned that the duel had been witnessed again. However, the train pulled into Helston railway station and Oates disembarked before he had time to elicit further confirmation from the anonymous clergyman.

The sighting of the duel was very close to the entrance to Bochym Manor, itself said to be haunted by two ghosts, although Jelf was not aware of this at the time. One spirit of Bochym is that of the 'pink lady', which stands less than 4ft tall and is thought to be the spirit of a child, while the other is an unidentified entity, which is said to gaze from an upstairs window. It has been suggested that the two duellists might have been the father and sweetheart of the 'pink lady'.

Chagford, Devon

Around 1570, Whiddon Park, near Chagford, was the seat of the Whiddon family, the grand house there having been created by Judge John Whiddon. It was from this manor that Mary, the daughter of the house, married on 11 October 1641.

Mary had previously been courting another man, who she jilted in favour of her husband-to-be. Her spurned lover was unbearably jealous and, as Mary's wedding drew near, his anger reached fever pitch and he would viciously malign her to anyone who could be persuaded to listen.

On the day of the wedding, Mary looked radiant as she walked up the aisle of Chagford Church to meet her groom. The ceremony over, the newly created husband and wife walked back down the aisle to the church steps. Suddenly, there was a loud bang and Mary crumpled to the floor, a bright red stain slowly spreading across the breast of her white silk wedding gown.

Her devastated husband sank to his knees and cradled his bride in his arms, but Mary died where she had fallen, shot by the jealous lover whose affections she had rejected.

Mary's body was buried beneath the chancel of the church, her last resting place marked by a stone slab set into the floor. Her epitaph reads:

Mary Whiddon, daughter of Oliver Whiddon, who died in 1641
Reader, would'st though know who here
is laid,
Behold a matron, yet a maid
A modest look, a pious heart
A Mary for the better part
But dry thine eyes, why wilt thou
weep
Such damselles doe not die, but
sleep.

Chagford, 1960s.
(Author's collection)

An interior view of Chagford Church. (Author's collection)

An exterior view of Chagford Church. (© N. Sly)

Mary's ghost is said to still wander within the churchyard and at Whiddon Park, dressed in a seventeenth-century wedding dress, especially around the time of her wedding anniversary.

In 1971, another daughter of the house was to be married at the same church and awoke on the morning of her wedding to find the apparition of a sad-looking woman in a period wedding dress standing in her bedroom doorway. On that occasion, the bride apparently placed her wedding bouquet on Mary Whiddon's grave as a mark of respect, something that has since been done by other brides marrying at the church.

It is said that the legend of Mary Whiddon was the inspiration for part of R.D. Blackmore's book *Lorna Doone*. The author is known to have spent some time in the Chagford area and it is almost certain that he was familiar with the story and that it inspired him to create a similar storyline.

Note: Both Whiddon Park and John Whiddon are sometimes spelled Whyddon in historical accounts.

Lizard Point, Cornwall

During the Second World War, many service men and women were stationed in Cornwall, among them was Corporal Joan Lewis from Porthcawl, who was billeted at the Housel Bay Hotel at Lizard Point. Twenty-seven-year-old Joan had been resident at the hotel for some months when a new station commander, Flying Officer William Croft, arrived.

Croft, who was five years older than Joan, was a married man from Bath and had two young children. In spite of this, he and Joan became close friends and their friendship soon blossomed into a passionate love affair.

Yet the relationship troubled Croft. He was not just committing adultery, but also engaging in fraternisation between the ranks, a practice very much frowned upon by the armed forces. Eventually, his guilty conscience prompted him to confide in Freda Catlin, the officer who was in charge of the WAAFs. Catlin advised him in no uncertain terms that the affair should stop immediately, since it was not conducive to either morale or discipline. Not only must the association cease but one of the couple must be reposted.

Arrangements were made for Joan Lewis to be moved to another station in Devon on Saturday 16 October 1943, but Croft found that he could hardly bear the prospect of being parted from her. In one of the many love letters to pass between the couple, Croft wrote: 'The thought of some other male sharing your company drives me to distraction. Please don't let us think of Saturday, Joan darling. I cannot dare to think of it. Every time, I get a horrible aching pain.'

Joan was permitted a couple of days leave before her transfer, which she spent with Croft, before returning to duty on 14 October. On the following day, she seemed quite cheerful, if resigned, and the couple spent that night together in a summerhouse in

Right: *Housel Bay Hotel, The Lizard. (Author's collection)*

Below: *Housel Bay and Lizard lighthouse. (Author's collection)*

the hotel garden. Towards dawn, the sound of two shots was heard coming from the summerhouse and, seconds later, Croft ran to the hotel, where he approached the duty officer and told him that he had killed Joan.

Charged with Joan's murder, Croft was later to say in court that the lovers had made a suicide pact. They had awakened in the summerhouse at about half-past four on a rainy, windy morning, on which the moon was obscured by clouds. Having spent their last night together talking, smoking and dozing, Croft now placed the gun on his lap and the pair agreed that whoever felt like making the first move would use the gun, leaving the survivor to follow. According to his confession, Croft fell asleep again, to be awakened by a loud bang. He saw Joan clasping her chest, complaining of pain and begging him to go and get help, at which he climbed out of the window and ran towards the hotel. He had no sooner set off, than he heard the second shot. Rushing

An artist's impression of the ghost of Joan Lewis.
(© Devon & Cornwall Constabulary)

back to the summerhouse, he snatched up the revolver and put it to his own head, but was unable to fire.

Croft was charged with Joan's murder and tried at Winchester Assizes. He was found guilty and sentenced to death, although his sentence was eventually commuted to one of life imprisonment and he was released from prison after serving just a few years of his sentence.

Meanwhile, several seemingly reliable witnesses, with no prior knowledge of the tragedy, have reported seeing a young woman sitting on a bench in the gardens of the Housel Bay Hotel. The woman, whose physical description tallies closely with that of Joan Lewis, wears a WAAF uniform and is always reported as either looking sad, or weeping. One witness, who was a spiritual medium, even managed to engage the young woman in 'conversation'. The medium was told that the young WAAF was waiting for her lover – who was also her murderer – to join her, as he had promised in a suicide pact, in 1943.

In recent years, there have been no further reported sightings of the ethereal woman on the bench. Is it possible that, so many years after her murder, she has finally been joined by her lover and is now able to rest in peace?

St Breock, Cornwall

Associated with the St Breock area is the legend of John (Jan) Tregeagle or Tregagle. Tales of Tregeagle's activities stretch the length and breadth of Cornwall, but he was apparently born at Trevorder near Wadebridge in the early part of the seventeenth century.

He died in October 1655 and was buried in St Breock churchyard, but his name has lived on through the centuries.

In life, Tregeagle was a cruel and dishonest magistrate who is supposed to have made his fortune by robbing the estate of an orphan, and who is rumoured to have murdered his wife and children. Legend has it that after his death, a bitter dispute arose between two Bodmin families over a parcel of land. One of the claimants to the ownership of the land had employed Tregeagle as a legal advisor, but had been defrauded when Tregeagle forged some papers. The dispute was brought to court and, at the point when all that remained was for the judge to summarise the case for the jury, one of the litigants asked for permission to call another witness. Permission was duly granted and, to the amusement of the spectators, the name 'Jan Tregeagle' was called. However, the laughter soon died down when the ghostly figure of the former magistrate manifested itself in the witness box.

The shadowy figure of Tregeagle testified to having deceived the defendant out of his rightful possession of the land. However, having been summoned to testify, when he had finished he was reluctant to leave the court and return to Hell.

It proved impossible to dismiss him from court hence it was decided to summon the clergy for assistance. Believing that it was their duty to save Tregeagle's soul, the priests determined that he should be set a series of seemingly impossible earthly tasks. The first of these was to empty Dozmary Pool on Bodmin Moor using only a holed limpet shell.

Dozmary Pool has associations with the legend of King Arthur. After Arthur was mortally wounded, his knight, Sir Bedivere, threw the king's sword, Excalibur, into the water where it was immediately reclaimed by the lady of the lake. At the time Tregeagle was set the task of emptying it, it was thought to be bottomless and to have links to the sea, beliefs that were disproved in the 1860s when the pool dried up completely. A host of hellhounds and demons waited to drag Tregeagle back to Hell, should he ever cease his attempts to empty the pool. His desperate screams of frustration at the impossibility of his task are said to echo across the moor.

Dozmary Pool. (Author's collection)

Yet, one night when the wind was especially fierce and the usually still waters of the pool were whipped into tremendous waves, Tregeagle seized the opportunity to escape and fled across the moors to Roche with the Devil's hounds in hot pursuit. Seeing the fourteenth-century chapel at Roche Rock, Tregeagle tried to fling himself through the stained-glass window to gain sanctuary. But while his head passed easily through the glass, his shoulders stuck, leaving his body outside to be savaged by the satanic dogs and demons.

His anguished screams caught the attention of a local priest who summoned forth two saints to capture the spirit of Jan Tregeagle and remove it. In various versions of the legend, Tregeagle is taken to either Padstow or Gwenvor Cove, where he was set the task of weaving a rope from beach sand.

He eventually succeeded in this task on a bitterly cold night, having poured water over his rope of sand so that it froze completely solid. However, he was quickly set the task of remaking the rope and this time forbidden to approach the water. On windy nights at Gwenvor, when the sand is scattered across the beach by gales, the noise of the wind is supposedly punctuated by howls from Tregeagle as he is thwarted in his task.

Other versions of the legend tell of Tregeagle being sent to Padstow, where he was set the same task. There, the local people grew tired of his unearthly cries and summoned St Petroc, who bound the spirit of Jan Tregeagle in chains and took him to Berepper, where he was set the task of carrying sand across the Loe Estuary to Portleven. His task would only be judged complete when the beach at Berepper was nothing more than bare rock, yet at every new tide, the sand moved by Tregeagle was replaced.

The Devil's minions were still lying in wait for his soul and, one night, when Tregeagle was crossing the estuary, one of the demons tripped him up causing him to spill his sack of sand, thus creating the dangerous Loe Bar sandbank. Furious at having their route from the harbour to the sea cut off, the local people summoned a priest, who banished Tregeagle to Land's End. Here he is still engaged in moving sand from Porthcurno Cove to Mill Bay and once again his task is made impossible by the tides, which replenish the sand at each turn.

Thus the howling gales that regularly sweep Cornwall are said by many to be interspersed with either the desperate screams of Jan Tregeagle, as he labours endlessly at his impossible tasks, or the frustrated howls of the army of demons who wait in vain to return his soul to Hell.

Torpoint, Cornwall

One of the strangest tales of ghostly activity is that of Antony House in Torpoint, since it involves the sighting of the ghost of a living person.

In October 1880, Lady Helen Waldegrave paid a visit to Antony House in Torpoint. She was accompanied by her maid, Helen Alexander. Helen was a quiet girl, who tended to keep herself to herself, hence the servants at Antony House knew very little about her.

While staying at Antony House, Helen Alexander fell ill with typhoid fever. Throughout Helen's illness, a maid from the house, Frances Reddel, was assigned to care for her. Several times, Frances inexplicably heard the sound of a bell ringing from the corridor outside the sick room, but simply assumed that there was some kind of malfunction in the system of bells installed to summon the house servants.

In the early hours of one morning, Frances happened to look up from preparing a dose of medicine for her charge and noticed a woman walk into the room, carrying an ornate brass candlestick and, without speaking, head straight for Helen's bedside. Much to her surprise, the woman appeared to be dressed in her nightclothes and Frances could even see a small hole in the red flannel petticoat that the stout elderly woman wore beneath her nightdress.

By the time Frances finished preparing the medicine for her patient, the woman had vanished as suddenly as she had appeared.

Helen had refused to write to her family during her illness, insisting that she didn't want anyone to worry about her. Now Frances noticed that Helen's condition was worsening and, although the doctor was called, the woman died within two hours of the visitation by the old lady.

When Helen's family arrived at Antony House for her funeral, Frances was shocked to see that Helen's mother was the double of the woman she had seen materialising at the sick girl's bedside just days earlier. Furthermore, in conversation with Helen's sister, Frances learned that Helen's mother owned a red flannel petticoat with a hole in it where her stays had worn through the material and also customarily carried a brass candlestick identical to the one carried by the apparition, even down to a small dent in its base.

Frances also discovered that, even though Helen's family did not know that she was gravely ill so many miles from home, the girl's mother had been inexplicably worried about her daughter and had experienced a strong sense of foreboding around the time of her apparent visitation to her daughter's bedside.

Antony House.
(Author's collection)

NOVEMBER

Aller, Devon

In the 1960s, newlyweds John and Carol Durston moved into the ground-floor flat at Aller House near Abbotskerswell. Within days, they found themselves plagued by a series of unnatural occurrences, which eventually led to the couple being too afraid to sleep in their own home.

Parts of the flat inexplicably remained icy cold, even when there was a fire burning in the grate. Furniture and ornaments were moved by unseen hands and, on one occasion, 'something' rolled up a rug as the terrified couple watched in disbelief. The whole flat echoed with the sound of heavy footsteps and a strange shuffling noise, sounds that were verified by the occupants of the other ground-floor flat, who reported being awakened several times by loud noises apparently emanating from the Durston's flat. Both John and Carol independently witnessed a mysterious white mist, which gradually formed itself into the recognizable shape of a plump man.

Eventually, after a particularly harrowing night of ghostly activity, the couple fled the flat in the early hours of the morning. Now desperate, they called in Revd Gordon Langford, the vicar of Abbotskerswell.

Langford visited the flat and although he personally could feel nothing unusual there, he agreed to investigate and discovered that the house had previously been used as the offices for a factory built behind it. The factory had been demolished in 1939, but there had apparently been two suicides recorded in the twentieth century, one of a factory employee and another actually in the Durston's flat, where a previous resident had hanged himself.

Langford reported his findings to Dr Mortimer, the Bishop of Exeter, who agreed to hold a special service at the flat. It was reported in *The Times* of 14 November 1963 that, during this service, the temperature in the room suddenly dropped alarmingly, leaving all present feeling as though they were standing in an icy wind.

According to *The Times*, the flat had been quiet since the bishop's visit. However, subsequent reports indicated that the ghost of the plump man had simply moved to another flat in the building and, within weeks, had apparently returned to haunt the Durstons. Perhaps not surprisingly, they moved out shortly afterwards.

Bolventor, Cornwall

Although Jamaica Inn at Bolventor was built in 1750, it remained a quiet coaching inn until it became associated with the writer Daphne Du Maurier. Du Maurier visited the inn in November 1930 and it became the inspiration for her book *Jamaica Inn*, which was first published in 1936.

The inn is said to be one of the most haunted pubs in Britain and, although I have been unable to identify any of the supposed ghosts by name, the reports of spirit activity are so frequent and so consistent that they merit inclusion here.

Left: *Jamaica Inn, Bolventor. (Author's collection)*

Below: *The lounge at Jamaica Inn. (Author's collection)*

THE LOUNGE, JAMAICA INN, BOLVENTOR.

The sign at Jamaica Inn, 1950s. (Author's collection)

The most frequently reported phenomena is the man who sits on the outside wall of the inn, seemingly oblivious to the sights and sounds of the twenty-first century going on all around him. He remains absolutely motionless, staring directly ahead and not responding to any attempts to communicate with him.

It is rumoured that, many years ago, a stranger to Cornwall stood at the bar drinking a tankard of ale. He was summoned outside and left his half-finished drink behind. His body was found the following morning on Bodmin Moor and, it is said, bears a strong physical likeness to the man who sits on the wall.

Countless people have heard footsteps walking through the inn when no one was in the vicinity and there have been numerous sightings of a cloaked man walking around the pub, who seems to be able to pass through locked doors.

There are unexplained cold spots throughout the pub and, before the ban on smoking in public houses came into being, smouldering cigarettes were found in clean ashtrays and waitresses claimed to have both smelled and seen cigarette smoke when there were no smokers present.

Conversations have been heard in the inn, although they have not been conducted in English – it is thought that the unseen speakers may be speaking in the ancient Cornish language.

A long-term employee at the inn, Reg Carthew, firmly believed that the building was haunted and admitted that he often felt a 'presence' as he was going about his work, particularly in the older parts of the inn, as though somebody was standing behind him watching his every move.

Other people claim to have heard the sounds of horses and carriages on the car park outside and some believe that they have heard the sound of laughing children. There is anecdotal evidence, which I have unfortunately been unable to verify, that the son of a former landlord disappeared from a child's birthday party that was taking place in the garden, in the early part of the twentieth century.

Kennall Vale, near Ponsanooth, Cornwall

Throughout most of the nineteenth century, the Kennall Vale was devoted to the production of gunpowder, for which there was a ready market in the numerous tin mines and stone quarries throughout Cornwall. The falling waters of the River Kennall powered the gunpowder mills, enabling the production of between 4,000 and 5,000 barrels of gunpowder every year.

Needless to say, it was a highly dangerous occupation and there were frequent accidents in the vale, in spite of strenuous efforts to create the safest possible conditions for the workers. More trees were planted throughout the area to try and maintain the moisture in the atmosphere and the complex of mills and workshops was specifically designed to incorporate firebreaks, with each building having a specially constructed roof that would blow cleanly off in the event of an explosion.

Nevertheless, there were frequent reports of accidents and fatalities in the contemporary local newspapers. In February 1826, a female employee was roasting potatoes and apparently singed her clothing. When she went into the mixing house, a spark from her dress ignited the gunpowder there, causing an explosion.

There was a further fatality in January 1841, when an unexplained explosion in the glossing mill literally blew worker John Martin to pieces. His head was found almost a quarter of a mile away from the heart of the explosion, which uprooted several nearby trees and shook houses for many miles around. The remains of poor John Martin were eventually collected together in a large sheet before being buried at Stithians churchyard.

An explosion on 3 May 1844 claimed the life of another worker, John Andrew, and, in 1853, fifty-six-year-old Samuel Peters committed suicide at his home in Ponsanooth, having been employed at the mills for almost thirty years.

However, the biggest explosion occurred in the press house at a few minutes past eight o'clock on the morning of 7 November 1887. Labourer James Paddy was working with a horse and cart, taking gunpowder to the building for pressing into cakes by hydraulic power. The process of dragging the barrels of gunpowder across the floor was believed to have created a spark, which ignited gunpowder dust in the bottom of the cart.

The horse was blown several yards across the valley but, apart from being slightly singed, escaped with just a small cut caused by a splinter of glass. James Paddy and William Dunstan, who was working in the press house at the time, were less fortunate.

Paddy was blown into a stream, 15yds from the press house and suffered severe burns as well as a broken arm and leg. He was rushed to Truro Royal Infirmary, where his leg was subsequently amputated. Paddy survived for only a few days after the operation.

At first, there was no trace of Dunstan, but eventually one of his legs was found under rubble, about 5yds from the press house. The rest of his body travelled almost 50yds before coming to rest under a bank. He left a wife and a large family of nine or ten children.

The mills eventually closed in 1914, after gelignite and dynamite largely replaced gunpowder in the mining and quarrying industries and made the gunpowder mills redundant. The buildings gradually fell into disrepair and the area is now a nature reserve. However, as might be expected in an area where so many violent deaths have occurred, it is reportedly not without the ghosts of its industrial past.

A man in old-fashioned clothing has been reported lurking around the ruined buildings, staring curiously at passers by, but vanishing if approached. It is said that strange, floating apparitions have been captured on film, while numerous people have experienced intense feelings of sadness.

Others talk of time slips and of suddenly seeing the complex of mills as it was at the peak of its production. Dogs have been known to behave strangely in the area, including my own Labrador, Wesley, who suddenly sat down mid-walk and refused to go a step further. His relief when we finally stopped trying to persuade him to move and turned back to the car was almost comical.

Wesley, the author's dog, who was sensitive to the atmosphere at Kennall Vale. (Author's collection)

Mevagissey, Cornwall

While driving one November afternoon, Mr Clifford Hocking came literally face-to-face with an apparition from the past.

En route from his home in Mevagissey to visit his wife in hospital in Truro, Mr Hocking was horrified to see a bright red stagecoach, pulled by four galloping horses, heading directly towards him at speed along the narrow country lane. The driver, who wore a wide-lapelled blue greatcoat, was urging the horses ever faster with his whip, while at his side, a man in a red coat and black hat frantically blew warning blasts on a horn.

A collision seemed inevitable and Mr Hocking could do little more than brace himself, burying his face in his hands as the coach barrelled towards him. Aware only of the sounds of the wheels on the lane, the thundering hooves of the horses and the blare of the horn, Mr Hocking waited for the stagecoach to impact his car. However, the anticipated crash never came and, as quickly as it had materialised, the stagecoach vanished.

Okehampton, Devon

At the end of November 1999, the owners of Okehampton railway station announced that, due to ill health, they were reluctantly putting the building up for sale. The station originally opened on 3 October 1871 but was closed in the 1970s after which it quickly fell into dereliction.

The *Western Morning News* reported on 6 December 1999 that the announcement of the intended sale of the carefully and lovingly restored station seemed to have upset the resident ghost, who was now very much in evidence after a previous period of inactivity lasting for several months.

Okehampton railway station. (© N. Sly)

'Sam', believed to be the spirit of a former train driver, was described as a 'mischievous ghost', who made his presence felt by rattling doors, throwing cups around and interfering with the coffee machine, making it click and tick.

Poughill, near Bude, Cornwall

The following account was related to me by a close friend, who has asked to remain anonymous. With his permission, I have been able to verify certain aspects of the story. I have checked with his employer who confirms that the telephone call to the police was made and that my friend was subsequently spoken to 'off the record' by the local policeman. However, I have been unable to trace details of any accident at the place he describes – therefore I will leave it to you, the reader, to make of it what you will.

I work as a herdsman and milk cows for a local dairy farmer every morning and evening. One November morning in 1999, I was driving to work at about 5 a.m. It was very dark and there were no streetlights, only the headlights of my car. There had been a very heavy frost overnight and the road sparkled with ice, hence I was driving particularly carefully as I knew that the roads were extremely slippery.

As I left the town of Bude and drove through Poughill, I suddenly saw a flash of white from the pavement out of the corner of my eye. Before I had a chance to react, a child ran out into the road a few yards in front of me and stood motionless directly in front of my car.

Poughill, near Bude, 1960s. (Author's collection)

An artist's impression of the Poughill apparition. (Drawing by Melanie Crawford)

It was a young girl, aged about ten or eleven. She was wearing a long, white nightdress and had dark hair, falling in loose curls to just above her waist. In a split second, I registered that she was barefoot.

I slammed the brakes on and the car skidded wildly on the icy road. By the time I had regained control, the little girl had vanished without a trace.

Although I hadn't felt any bumps, I got out and checked all around the car and also underneath it. I called out 'Hello' a couple of times, followed by 'Do you need any help?' but there was no response, so I could do little else but continue driving to work.

However, the barefoot girl preyed on my mind. Even if I hadn't hit her, the idea of a young child running around without shoes, wearing just a flimsy nightdress on such a bitterly cold morning worried me and, by the time I got to work ten minutes later, I had decided to ring the police, just to be on the safe side. They took my details and promised to have a look round, telephoning me later that day to report that they had been unable to find any trace of a child in the area.

A couple of days afterwards, one of the local policemen rang and asked if he could speak to me 'off the record'. He told me that several years previously, a young girl lived in a cottage on my route to work and that, in the early hours of one morning, she had fled her drunken and abusive father, run out into the road and been killed by a passing vehicle.

At the time, my friend didn't think to ask the officer any details, so I have no clues to the child's name or the year of her death – if indeed she ever existed. One thing that I do know is that my friend never drove the same way to work again, preferring to take a much longer route rather than chance another encounter with the barefoot girl.

Torquay and St John's Church, 1920s. (Author's collection)

Torquay, Devon

On 19 November 1883, Henry Ditton-Newman died at the age of thirty-nine from pleurisy and was subsequently buried in Torquay Cemetery. Ditton-Newman was the organist at St John's Church in Torquay and had, over the course of his lifetime, composed several hymns, a collection of which were published after his death.

It is reported that, at the organist's funeral, the organ played by itself, and this incident seems to have been the start of a long series of ghostly manifestations associated with the former organist who, it seems, was determined to complete some of his unfinished compositions and refused to let his premature death stand in the way of his goal.

The shadowy form of a man was frequently seen in the vicinity of the organ and, in 1959, the then vicar, the Revd Anthony Rouse, admitted that he had heard organ music coming from the completely empty church on numerous occasions. 'The organ made an extraordinary noise and the presence of the former organist was felt by everybody,' said Rouse, speaking of a rehearsal of the local choral society, which had to be abandoned when the organ suddenly began to play without the assistance of any worldly organist.

A report in the *Guardian* newspaper of 22 January 1959 states that the organist at the time had been so affected by the ghostly presence that he had left the church and declined to take his seat at the organ again until he could be sure that it had been completely vacated by his predecessor. The newspaper reported that a letter had been written to the Bishop of Exeter, begging him to intervene.

St John's Church, Torquay. (Author's collection)

Later that year, the organ at St John's was replaced and, from then onwards, the appearances of Ditton-Newman at the church gradually declined. However, Montpelier House, the former vicarage and choir school of St John's, often visited by Ditton-Newman, was also said to be haunted by ghostly footsteps, although these have also been attributed to the ghost of a young man whose suicide at the house in 1953 I have been unable to verify.

Torre Abbey, Torquay, Devon

Torre Abbey was constructed in 1196 and in 1930 was offered for sale to Torbay Council for £40,000 by its then owners the Cary family. At least three active ghosts came with the purchase.

The first is said to roam the lanes around the nearby village of Torre, usually at around midnight during the month of November. It stems from a dispute between the villagers and the monastery in 1390, as a result of which the villagers began to spread vicious rumours about Abbot William Norton, the main one being that he had beheaded a young canon, Simon Hastings, in a fit of temper.

The gossip reached the ears of Bishop Brantingham of Exeter who immediately visited the abbey to investigate the stories for himself. On his arrival, Abbot Norton introduced him to a young man, who he said was Simon Hastings, satisfying the bishop that the rumours were unfounded. However, many villagers refused to be

Torre Abbey. (Author's collection)

An interior view of Torre Barn. (Author's collection)

An exterior view of Torre Barn. (© N. Sly)

convinced and insisted that they had seen the young man's headless ghost, galloping on his horse through the lanes.

The second ghost of Torre Abbey is believed to be a previous Lady Cary, who appears in a brightly lit carriage driving through the abbey grounds, dressed in a ball gown as if heading to a function.

However, perhaps the most famous ghost of Torre Abbey is the so-called 'Spanish Lady'. In 1588, Sir Francis Drake's ship *Revenge* captured the *Nuestra Senora del Rosario*, a ship from the Spanish Armada. The crippled Spanish ship was towed into Torbay and its crew was taken to Torre Abbey, where they were imprisoned in the old tithe barn.

One of the captured sailors was in fact a woman, the fiancée of one of the Spanish lieutenants. Unwilling to be parted from her fiancé, the young woman quickly disguised herself as a man. However, she caught a chill and died and her true gender was not discovered until after her death.

Since then, her unhappy ghost is said to haunt the barn and the grounds around it, sobbing quietly as she searches endlessly for her lost lover.

DECEMBER

Bude, Cornwall

In December 2006, Karen and her children moved into a brand new house on an estate in Bude, Cornwall.

Almost immediately, Karen began to notice strange smells in the home, particularly the smell of aftershave and the distinctive odour of a match that has just been struck. Before long, the family began to notice unexplained cold spots in the master bedroom and also to experience many strange electrical phenomena.

The television repeatedly switched itself on, as did the touch-sensitive lights in the bedroom. Some electrical items, such as hair clippers, inexplicably temporarily stopped working. Items were also moved around in the kitchen – often, things disappeared and then unexpectedly reappeared later, in plain view on the work surfaces.

Karen's young daughter talked repeatedly of seeing a face in the window. One day, while looking through an old photograph album, she excitedly pointed to a picture of a man, telling her mother, 'That's him. That's the man in my window.'

The picture was one of Karen's grandfathers, who the little girl had not known at all when he was alive.

Housing estate, Bude, Cornwall. (© N. Sly)

Bude, Cornwall, 1960s.
(Author's collection)

Karen eventually had a sitting with a nationally known medium and described her reading as 'impressively accurate'. Karen felt that the medium had given her a lot of personal information, naming a lot of names and imparting many personal details, of the kind that would simply not be known to a stranger.

It appears that whoever or whatever is making its presence known to Karen – probably her grandparents – is entirely personal to her. Karen and her family have not inadvertently moved into a so-called 'haunted house', but apparently the spirits of those people whom she loved in life have taken it upon themselves to look over her and her family after their deaths.

Exeter, Devon

There has been an inn on the site of the Prospect Inn on the quayside in Exeter for around 200 years. Each year, on Christmas Day, a little girl dressed in Victorian costume and clutching a rag doll supposedly visits one of the upstairs rooms. The child smiles gently at anyone who sees her before gradually fading away.

The pub also boasts a very active poltergeist in the cellar, which spins beer barrels and makes repeated tapping sounds.

Kingsbridge, Devon

In December 2004, the quarterly newsletter issued by the Kingsbridge Town Council relates that the Urban District Council used to be housed in a building on Fore Street in Kingsbridge.

The offices had a resident ghost, which the caretaker, Harry, apparently saw on several occasions. A headless nun would often walk up the stairs from the basement boiler room, always followed by a dog.

Kingsbridge, 1920s. (Author's collection)

The building was known to have historical connections with nearby Buckfast Abbey, a place not without its own ghostly association as it formerly housed 'Drake's Drum'.

The drum, said to have been owned by Sir Francis Drake, is reputed to sound whenever England is in peril or has defeated an enemy. The drum has 'spoken' on numerous occasions since the sixteenth century, including at the outbreak of both the First and Second World Wars, the Falklands War and most recently on 7 July 2005, when London was hit by terrorist bombings.

The drum was rescued from a fire at the abbey in 1939 and moved to its present home at the Buckland Abbey Maritime Museum near Yelverton.

Launceston, Cornwall

Nicholas Herle was a noted barrister who served as both the High Sheriff and the Mayor of Launceston, holding the latter office twice. He lived with his wife Elizabeth at Dockacre, a sixteenth-century mansion in Launceston.

After the tragic death of the couple's baby daughter, Henrietta, Elizabeth became deranged and Nicholas, who had himself begun drinking heavily after the tragedy, locked her in an upstairs room of the house. At the time, one of the prescribed cures for madness was starvation and it seems as if Elizabeth was deliberately kept without food. A monument in the Church of St Mary Magdalene refers to her as having died by 'starvation or other unlawful means'.

Buckfast Abbey. (Author's collection)

Drake's Drum, 1950s. (Author's collection)

Dockacre Road, Launceston. (© N. Sly)

On Christmas Day 1714, Elizabeth managed to break free from her prison and ran downstairs in an attempt to escape the house. As she descended the stairs, Nicholas shot her, either by accident or deliberately. Although the staircase of the house has long since been replaced, it is said that the original one, on which Elizabeth died, had an indelible bloodstain on the second tread, which no amount of cleaning would remove.

Nicholas eventually moved to London and died in Hampstead in 1728. Even so, his ghost was said to haunt Dockacre House, playing a flute whenever a death was about to occur in the house. Elizabeth too has also been seen, wearing a grey dress and looking unaccountably happy.

Previous owners of the house have reported unexplained footsteps, rattling and banging noises, pictures falling from the walls and doors opening and closing. Visitors to the house, unaware of its history, have reported feeling cold and faint in the vicinity of the stairs. One former occupant was the Revd Baring-Gould, who included the ghost of Dockacre in his book, *John Herring*.

It has also been a tradition for each successive owner of the house to present the new owner with a walking stick and it has been said that the sticks must be kept in a certain order. If they are moved, they will unaccountably rearrange themselves.

However, it appears that both Nicholas Herle and his wife Elizabeth are now at peace, since there have been no reported manifestations in recent years.

St Mary Magdalene Church, Launceston, where there is a monument to Elizabeth Herle. (Author's collection)

Lynmouth, Devon

On 10 December 1816, the lifeless body of an unidentified young woman was pulled from the Serpentine in Hyde Park, London. *The Times* reported that the woman, who wore an expensive ring on her finger, was far advanced in pregnancy. She was later identified as twenty-one-year-old Harriet, the estranged wife of poet Percy Bysshe Shelley.

Harriet had met Shelley after befriending his younger sister, Helen, at a girl's school in Clapham. Percy described her as having, 'a brilliant pink and white complexion and hair light brown' and, shortly after her sixteenth birthday, the couple eloped to Scotland. After their hasty marriage, sixteen-year-old Harriet and nineteen-year-old Percy honeymooned in Dublin and Wales before visiting Lynmouth in North Devon.

They spent an idyllic summer there in 1812, staying at Woodbine Cottage, which is now renamed Shelley's Cottage in their honour. However, in the winter of that year, Percy and his young bride returned to London, where the relationship between them quickly soured. One of the main causes of arguments between them was Harriet's older sister, Eliza, who had accompanied them on their honeymoon and had apparently caused Harriet to become jealous.

On 24 March 1814, Harriet and Percy went through a second marriage ceremony at St George's of Hanover Square. By now, the couple had a daughter, Eliza Ianthe, and there were doubts about the legitimacy of their Scottish wedding. Yet, with things far from happy at home, Percy began to absent himself more and more frequently,

Above: *The Serpentine, Hyde Park, 1909. (Author's collection)*

Left: *Shelley's Cottage, Lynmouth, 1927. (Author's collection)*

Lynmouth. (Author's collection)

spending time with intellectual William Godwin and his circle of literary friends. Four months after their second wedding ceremony, Harriet moved to Bath and the couple never lived together again.

Meanwhile, the temptation of Godwin's sixteen-year-old daughter, Mary, proved irresistible for Percy and soon the couple had run off to Europe together, leaving Harriet pregnant with the Shelley's second child. When Percy and Mary returned, she too was pregnant.

Percy gave Harriet a generous sum of money and she returned to live with her father for a while. She went on to take several lovers and, by 1816, had fallen pregnant once more. In shame, she moved out of her father's home, taking lodgings under the assumed name of Harriet Smith.

By November of 1816, Harriet was near to her confinement and desperately unhappy. On 9 November, she disappeared, having first written letters of farewell to her father, sister and husband:

My dear Bysshe, let me conjure you by the remembrance of our days of happiness to grant my last wish. Do not take your innocent child from Eliza who has been more than I have, who has watched over her with such unceasing care. Do not refuse my last request. I never could refuse you & if you had never left me I might have lived, but as it is I freely forgive you & may you enjoy that happiness which you have deprived me of.

Harriet's only true happiness in her tragically short life had been the period that she spent with her beloved husband at Lynmouth and it is said that, to this day, she walks the cottage trying to recapture those special days.

Pendeen, Cornwall

A souterrain is an underground chamber or passage, often dating back to the Iron Age or before. The name given to such structures in Cornwall is a fogou, thought to originate from the Cornish language for cave. Nobody is quite sure why fogous were built, although it has been suggested that they might have been used either for food storage or for defence purposes.

The fogou at Pendeen Manor Farm is quite extensive. The entrance, which is not original, leads to a downward sloping passage roughly 7m in length. To the northwest is a further passage some 10m long, while to the northeast is a chamber. Legend has it that the passage once extended to the sea, with some accounts even saying that it ran beneath the sea to the Scilly Isles, which lie some twenty-eight miles off the Cornish coast.

The Pendeen fogou has its own ghost; a White Lady is said to appear at the entrance to the fogou on Christmas morning, a red rose held in her mouth. Some accounts of the manifestation say that those who see the white lady are doomed to die within a year. Others say that, if she is followed into the fogou, the White Lady will transform into a terrifying, monstrous, malevolent form once inside.

Poundstock, Cornwall

In December of 1356, the mass being held at the tiny Church of St Winwaloe at Poundstock, to celebrate the Feast of St John the Apostle, was suddenly interrupted by a gang of men who rampaged through the small church, hacking at everything and everyone that stood in their way. In the course of the skirmish, William Penfound was slain on the chancel steps.

Penfound is variously described in different accounts of the incident as being either the vicar or the parish clerk of the church. The gang of men who slaughtered him were never identified, but were referred to as 'satellites of Satan' in the following statement, issued after the murder by the then Bishop of Exeter:

> Certain satellites of Satan, names unknown, on the Feast of St John the Apostle – which makes the crime worse – broke into the Parish Church of Poundstock within our Diocese with a host of armed men, during Mass, and before Mass was scarcely completed they furiously entered the Chancel and with swords and staves cut down William Penfound, clerk. Vestments and other Church Ornaments were desecrated with human blood in contempt of the Creator, in contempt of the Church, to the subversion of ecclesiastical liberty and the disturbance of the peace of the realm. Where will we be safe from crime if the Holy Church, our Mother, the House of God and the Gateway to Heaven is thus deprived of its sanctity?

St Winwaloe Church, Poundstock. (Author's collection)

An interior view of St Winwaloe Church, Poundstock. (© N. Sly)

The ghost of William Penfound can allegedly still be seen pottering about the church and churchyard as if continuing to carry out his clerical duties.

He had also been known to visit his family home, Penfound Manor, mentioned elsewhere in this book as the site of spectral visits by Kate Penfound, her father Arthur and her lover John Trebarfoot.

St Just, Cornwall

On 21 December 1783, widower John Thomas of Sancreed made one of his regular visits to the pub at St Just. Having imbibed a large quantity of alcohol, he was making his unsteady way home across the fields in the dark when he accidentally fell into a clay pit.

When Thomas didn't arrive home as expected, his disappearance was reported and a search was instigated, but no trace was found of the missing sixty-four-year-old man. However, exactly a week after his disappearance, James Thethewy was out searching for some missing sheep when he spotted the figure of a man standing at the edge of the clay pit.

As Thethewy drew nearer, the strange man walked around the top of the clay pit to the opposite side and then vanished. Curious, Thethewy approached the pit and heard a faint voice coming from the depths.

Thethewy was so frightened that he immediately fled. When he plucked up sufficient courage to return to the scene some time later, he again heard the weak voice and found his missing friend and neighbour John Thomas lying, injured but alive, at the bottom of the 30ft deep shaft. Thomas had survived by drinking the standing water at the pit bottom.

Several other local people had apparently seen the mysterious figure circling the entrance to the pit shaft in the preceding days, but all had been too afraid to investigate the apparition more closely.

Wadebridge, Cornwall

The Molesworth Arms Hotel at Wadebridge is a sixteenth-century coaching inn. At midnight on 31 December, a phantom coach and horses, driven by a headless horseman, is said to manifest in the courtyard and drive out of the inn at full speed. Some people claim to have actually seen the coach, others to have heard but not seen it. Yet others have neither seen nor heard the apparition but claim to have felt unaccountably apprehensive and to have somehow sensed its presence, without any prior knowledge of the legend. Similar sightings have been reported at nearby Trewornan Bridge, although in this instance a specific date is not given, as the apparition tends to appear when the moon is full. Another phantom coach and horses with a headless driver is said to drive through the town of Penryn, again in December, just before Christmas.

BIBLIOGRAPHY

Books

Anonymous, *The Famous Jamaica Inn* (Torquay; Hamilton Fisher & Co.)
Smit, T. *The Lost Gardens of Heligan* (London; Indigo, 2000)

Newspapers and Magazines

Bonhams Magazine
Cornish Guardian
Daily Mail
Exeter Flying Post
Guardian
Manchester Guardian
Plymouth Herald
Sun
Sunday Express
Taunton Courier
Telegraph
The Times
West Briton
Western Morning News

Website

www.oldbaileyonline.org

INDEX